Incident at the Historical Museum

LAWRENCE A. DEIMAN

First Edition

PAGE PUBLISHING, INC.
Conneaut Lake, PA

First originally published by Page Publishing 2020

ISBN 978-1-6624-0826-7 (pbk)
ISBN 978-1-6624-3038-1 (hc)
ISBN 978-1-6624-0827-4 (digital)

Printed in the United States of America

I dedicate this book to friends who lived these pages with me. To these friends (you know who you are), thanks for the memories!

A special thank-you to my mother and father for giving me the kind of life that allowed me to tell my stories with the warmth of their love! We love you and miss you each and every day. God will be at your side always with the deepest of love.

Chapter One

Wow, thinks Trevor Andrews after waking up next to Lois and finding out she was not the beauty that he thought she was when he picked her up at the bar last night, *too many drinks, I guess.*

Trevor says to Lois, "I really have to get to work. Can I drop you off somewhere?"

Lois replies, "It's Saturday. You work on Saturday?"

A stunned Trevor says, "I forgot its Saturday, but yeah, I need to go to the office today, just for a few hours. I need to take care of something important."

Trevor works for a government agency that provides intelligence information for the CIA, the FBI, and occasionally the NCIS. Mostly for the FBI though. Trevor wishes he could be a spy like some of those operatives that come in from time to time.

When he was a kid, he used to read all the spy books and magazines and would just be completely immersed in them and lose himself in the characters. How he ended up working for a company that is so closely related is just pure luck. He is basically a computer geek that runs numbers for the intelligence community.

"So is that a yes?" asks Trevor. "I really need to be there soon."

Trevor is afraid that he won't get there before the others in the office get there and that he won't be able to do what needs to be done. You never know who's going to show up at work on a Saturday.

Lois takes the ride and asks to be let off downtown. She will walk the rest of the way since he is in such a hurry.

Could've used a little less attitude from her, but oh well, Trevor thinks. He will probably never see her again.

After dropping her off, he finally gets to the office and finishes up what needs to be done before the weekend is over. Trevor is a third-level programmer who writes the programs for the missile launch platforms. They are doing a huge project for the Navy right now with some very strict deadlines. Now that he is done with this part of the project, he can take the rest of the weekend off.

Washington, DC, is so nice this time of year. He can catch up with his friend, Jason. Trevor, being 5 ft., 11 in. tall, 178 lb., and very good-looking makes him a real babe magnet, at least that's what Jason calls him. Jason is not so bad himself, being 6 ft., 1 in. tall, 197 lb., and all muscle. His physique always complements Trevor's, and when it comes to getting girls, they never have a problem. It's just a matter of picking a new one out every day, if they wanted.

Jason Brandt works in a different area from Trevor, but in some far-fetched way, it's kind of the same. He works in security. It's been many years since he has had a job that wasn't related in some way to security.

It wasn't always easy for Jason. He had a rough life growing up. He had a mother that was forced to choose between her new husband and her son. She chose her new husband and threw Jason out of the house when he was sixteen. He turned into a gutter rat and stayed that way for years. He had to steal from convenience stores so he could eat. He would get odd jobs just to survive. Trevor didn't know him then, but he had been hearing the story of his growing up for years. He started out in security for loss prevention at a department store and found he was really good at it. He ended up having the best record of their entire division in Maryland. He met Donald Vernon from Chevron when he came into the store, shopping one day, and they started talking. The next morning, Donald Vernon called Jason and offered him a job. He started working for him part-time and eventually started doing more and more until Donald Vernon hired him full-time. Of course, it wasn't Chevron when he started. It was Chancellor Security.

During his long career at Chevron, he eventually became indispensable to Mr. Vernon. He was promoted to operations manager after about five years or so. His new duties included running the company so Mr. Vernon could finally take a back seat to the operation and so he could spend more time with his family and enjoy the fruits of his labor. After all, he felt that the company was in good hands.

Jason could not have been happier. Jason ran the company successfully for about five to six years until one day, Mr. Vernon, without even discussing with Jason, hired a president to run the company instead of him and made this new president Jason's boss. Jason became disgruntled and tried speaking to Mr. Vernon about it. He tried to understand why he made this change. The company had never been more successful. Mr. Vernon never really gave him an answer, just that this was the way he wanted it and he would have to live with it.

Donald Vernon dismissed him, saying, "Oh well, decisions been made, and I am not changing it now. Besides, I have already hired Jesse."

Jason felt like he had been punched in the gut. He felt so betrayed. He called up Trevor and told him what was going on, and Trevor, being the great friend that he was, told him to meet him at their favorite bar. He needed cheering up.

Trevor said "Besides, maybe we can go home with some cute honeys tonight. That will really cheer you up."

Trevor got there first getting them a table. "Jason, over here. I ordered you a drink. Look at those two at the bar. They watched you come in, and that blonde one can't keep her eyes off you. Come on, let's ask them over. You could get lucky tonight. You'll forget all about this horrible business at work. Besides, I have an idea for you. I know how you can get out of Chevron and start on your own or at least get something going for yourself. I am not going to tell you about it tonight. Meet me tomorrow at the club, and I will introduce you to your future. Tonight… we party."

That was all Trevor was going to say about it. At least that's all he was going to say that night. The blonde at the bar trapped Jason at the entrance to the bathroom about thirty minutes later and asked if he would like to buy her a drink. He looked like he could use another one. Her name was Jeanette, and she had a great figure that even in this blue mood, Jason could not pass up. What Jason didn't know was that Trevor, having such a dictionary full of hot women, set it up for Jeanette to be there tonight to take Jason's mind off his troubles. It worked so well that Jason took her home after several drinks at the bar. A budding romance started. What Jason didn't know was that Jeanette is a hooker—a very expensive high-priced hooker. It cost a lot for Trevor to get her there, but the plan worked. Although Trevor didn't expect it to become more than that.

It was the break of a lifetime. He would be able to fulfill his dreams and finally be a business owner in the only business he knows, security. He owes his future to Trevor. Trevor was approached by a competitor of the company Jason was working for and was offered a partnership in the company. Jason and Trevor moved in the same groups, so it was an opportunity that was presented for Jason, not Trevor. Trevor was just asked to bring the idea to Jason. Jason doesn't know much of anything else, but he knows security and is very good at it. It wasn't until several months later that he found out his partner, Jeremy, was not to be trusted and was stealing from the company.

Jason and Trevor met in 1992 when they were both in college. Trevor defended Jason's honor at a get-together, and from that day on, Trevor and Jason have been the best of friends. Trevor worked many years for a corporate giant in the Maryland area. He was very good at what he did there until the company decided he was not worth all the money he was getting paid for and, like so many others, was laid off. After all, they could hire younger and more innovative college grads to do his job for a lot less.

After being laid off, Trevor was unemployed for a few months until he landed a job that was more suited to his talents. That's when he went to work for Consolidated Engineering. It is an all right job. He had the talent, and he was voted the most likely to end up in a geeky job from his college days. Trevor has several degrees that made him the perfect candidate for this position. So he writes programs that someone else takes credit for. It's not a perfect job, but they pay him a lot of money to do it that he can live with someone else taking the credit. The only catch is, he has to work in Washington, DC. He mentioned this to Jason, who was already thinking about moving there himself. This new opportunity is in the Maryland area.

Trevor, after finishing up his work on Saturday, decides to go spend time with his favorite girl at home, his beautiful dog, Jasmine. Unfortunately, he has been spending some long days and nights at work because of these damn deadlines, so he has been neglecting her. He walks through the front door to an excited Jasmine jumping up all over him. She was mad at him when he left this morning, but like most dogs, as soon as she sees her master, the anger or disappointment goes away and her tail is just wagging so fast she can knock you over. She's so happy to see him.

"Hello, baby. How's my girl?"

After calming her down and petting and caressing her, he grabs her leash and says, "Come on, girl. Let's go for a walk."

He takes her to her favorite place in Washington, West Potomac Park on Constitution Avenue. There's a male dog, Buster, that he thinks she likes and seems to always be there when they are, so the two of them play together. She plays, and Trevor sits with Buster's master on a park bench, watching them.

I have to admit, Trevor thinks, *I like going there to so I can see his master too.*

Trevor enjoys spending time with him. His master is a very handsome man that has this magnetism about him. He stands at six feet, two inches of cuteness, with huge biceps and six-pack abs. They have become friendly over the past few weeks that they have been coming here. He has an interesting job; he works at the historical museum as a junior curator. His name is Christopher—not Chris, Christopher. He corrected Trevor on that the first day they met.

"You know, Trevor," says, Christopher, "since we have the dogs in common and we seem to get along so well ourselves, why don't we meet up sometime without the dogs and get to know each other even better?"

"I would like that," Trevor responds. "Maybe you can give me a private tour at the historical museum. Since I moved here, I have yet to find the time to check it out. I know it takes a really long time to see it all, but I can be patient." Trevor flashes a mischievous grin and adds playfully, "I am also a really good cook. In fact, I am a gourmet. Maybe sometime we could have dinner at my place."

"I would really like that," Christopher responds with a kind of shyness that makes Trevor smile.

"In fact, I am not doing anything tonight. If you would be interested in coming over and hanging out with me and Jasmine,". says Trevor, not wanting to push him into anything but really wanting to hook up sooner than later.

"Damn, I wish I could, but I have the late shift tonight. Say, I have an idea. Why don't you come over to the museum tonight after it closes? And I can give you that private tour—that is, if it's not too late for you. We can start our tour at the historical museum information center in the main building. That's where all the information is on the historical museum and the perfect place to start. It closes at five thirty p.m. My shift starts at six p.m., so I can meet you at the employee's entrance at about eight, giving me time to get some of my stuff done before you get there—"

Trevor interrupts, "Are you sure it's all right to be there after hours? I don't want to get you into trouble or anything."

"No, its fine," Christopher says. "Employees do it all the time. As long as we get our work done, they don't care. It's kind of a perk. Probably makes up for the lousy wages. So what do you say?"

Trevor is excited by the prospect of seeing the historical museum, or at least part of it after hours when there are no other visitors. "I would love to. Let's do it."

The historical museum is comprised of several museums and several parks in Washington, DC. Most museums are open daily from 10:00 a.m. to 5:30 p.m., except December 25. The historical museum offers endless opportunities to stimulate the imaginations of growing minds.

Trevor arrives at the employee entrance, following Christopher's directions and finding it with no problem. It is about ten minutes before 8:00 p.m., so Trevor waits outside for Christopher to come out and get him. At 8:00 p.m. sharp, Christopher opens the door and waves him in. When he gets in, he thinks that he was going to get a guided tour, but Christopher had other ideas on his mind apparently. As they walk through the first room, which showed a layout of the first museum, Christopher starts getting really close to Trevor and starts talking really soft like he is trying to keep from being heard by others.

"Trevor, I know that we have not known each other for very long, but I really feel we have a connection. A sort of affection for each other. I know you have felt it too. I would really like to pursue a relationship with you."

Christopher was talking really fast. He seems nervous, as though he planned or rehearsed what he was going to say. Trevor is really surprised by this, not that he was not thinking of the same thing. It's just that he seemed bold to blurt it out almost as soon as they got inside.

Trevor puts his hand on Christopher's and says, "I do feel the same, and I would really like to pursue a relationship with you too. I think since you are working tonight, I should probably go and let you finish your work, and we can get together another time, maybe tomorrow."

"Yeah, that's fine. Probably wouldn't remember much anyway. I am so distracted right now," Christopher responds. He reaches over and kisses Trevor on the cheek before he loses his nerve.

While driving home, Trevor is wondering if he will be able to keep this secret. He has had these feelings for a long time, but he kind of pushed them away and denied his feelings. But this new development presents a bit of a challenge. He has to be very careful because Jason doesn't know that Trevor is gay. He will freak out if he finds out. He will have to be careful. This is the first time that he was actually presented with this dilemma, especially since he really likes this guy. He has never felt this way about another person before. Well, he will just see where it goes and then worry about it later. Right now, he is going to go home and snuggle up with a good book with Jasmine at his side.

Chapter Two

Jason is having a great time with Jeanette.

Man, is she hot, he thinks.

Jason caresses her thighs and slowly helps her out of her top which reveals no bra. Her breasts pop out and just bounces a little until Jason gets his hands on them. He puts one hand on each, licking ever so lightly the nipple on her left breast and then doing the same on the right nipple, nice and slow and ever so soft, in a way that is driving Jeanette crazy. Her nipples get very hard and stand straight out, nearly poking Jason in the eye. He can't believe how incredible she looks. By this time, Jason is so hard that he can't stand it. He feels he is going to pop his cork before he even gets it out of his pants. Jeanette, seeing this huge throbbing lump in his pants, slowly moves her mouth to Jason's now damp jeans. His obvious arousal puts a mischievous grin on her face. Jeanette starts caressing his member until Jason finally stops her.

"Hey, baby, you're going make me explode before we even get started. Let's get out of these clothes and then we can really enjoy ourselves."

Jeanette says, "Okay, sweetie, but I get to take your clothes off and *you* can finish taking off mine."

Jason finishes taking her clothes off with his teeth. He carefully grabs her jeans, and after unbuttoning them, he grabs them with his teeth and starts moving them down Jeanette's beautiful figure, stopping at her vagina to take in the incredible smell that envelopes his mind and body. In fact, it occupies every fiber of his being and makes him even harder, if that is possible. He is so ready to burst right now. When he finally gets to slide his penis in, he will explode after only a couple of strokes. No woman has ever made him feel this way, at least not for a long time.

He finally gets her pants off and then her perfumed panties. Now she lies on his bed with her legs spread and with that delightful, ever so soft and tender spot that he loves so much—a crease that is so wet it almost spreads itself in the longing of his member that is now inches away from her. Jason's member is so stiff and throbbing to the point that the head is of a purplish color with some juices oozing out of it still. He wants so badly to jump on her and just start making love to her until they both explode in a symphony of lust and desire.

Jeanette slowly touches his member and starts caressing it ever so lightly until he puts his hand on hers and says, "It's now or never. I am ready to explode all over this place. I want to jump on you right now."

Jeanette very softly with her finger in her mouth, she licks her finger and moves it in and out, in and out. Jason slides on a condom and enters her lips of desire and starts sliding it in and out of her tender spot, moving it nice and slow in order to savor the essence of the moment.

Jeanette screams, "Oh my god… oh Jason, harder, harder!"

Jason plunges into her harder than he has ever done before.

In a loud scream from both of them, Jason screams, "Oh my god!"

He explodes in Jeanette, which seems like forever and feels like gallons. He finally is totally spent, and Jeanette is lying on the bed completely out of breath. They both just lie there, breathless, and taking in the aroma of what just transpired. Then they fall asleep in each other's arms.

Chapter Three

Trevor wakes up the next morning hungry, realizing he forgot to eat dinner last night.

Oh well, he thinks to himself, *I will get something to eat later when I meet up with Jason. He is probably really curious about this deal I have for him. I hope he at least takes the time to look into it because I don't like seeing him so unhappy. What the hell was Vernon thinking of when he fucked Jason like that? Something must have happened that Jason isn't saying. Oh well, it's probably time for him to move on anyway.*

After putting Jasmine out in the backyard, Trevor looks in the kitchen for something to chew on until he has to leave. Opening the fridge, he realizes he forgot to go grocery shopping this week. He has nothing to eat. No eggs, cereal, nothing. Jasmine is also almost out of food.

If I don't eat, at least I have to feed her, Trevor thinks. *Oh well, I'll call Jason and set up a time and then go take a shower.*

Trevor reaches for the phone to call him. "Jason, you up? Just wondering when you want to meet up. I just want to introduce you to Jeremy and then let you two talk it over and see if you can come up with a plan of action that will make you both happy and hopefully rich someday."

"I had a great night last night, Trevor," Jason says wearily. He hasn't really woken up yet. "I met this girl, Jeanette. Damn, what a fox. I am just waking up now."

Jason gets out of bed to start some coffee. "Maybe that'll wake me up some," Jason thinks out loud, just barely for Trevor to hear.

Trevor says, "I told Jeremy I would call him this morning, which, by the way, is almost over."

"Why don't you call him and call me back? I need to take a shower," Jason states. "Set it up and call me in about twenty minutes. By then, I will at least get my shower done. Where are we meeting him? Have you set up a place yet?"

"Not yet," Trevor says, "but it will probably be at some local lounge or restaurant. I will set it all up before I let him go. Want me to pick you up on the way?"

"No, I think you should make the introductions and then bow out after a few minutes," Jason says. "I know what I want, and if this guy can deliver or at least show me this is a good deal, I will probably want to discuss specifics which would be boring for you."

"Fine. I will call you in twenty." Trevor hangs up and calls Jeremy. He sets up the meeting with him for 2:00 p.m. this afternoon and gives Jason some time to get out of the shower before he calls him back. It gives him time to take a shower himself.

Jeremy Blackstone is an interesting character. He owned a company once before that went bankrupt. Jeremy is a black man with a major chip on his shoulder. He was a cop once, which ended very badly. After fifteen years in the Memphis police force, he was caught up in a sting operation that ended his career. He was accused of taking kickbacks on several levels. He was accused of stealing drugs that were apparently taken from drug busts he was in charge of. He would only report certain amounts of the drugs seized but not the entire amount. No one was the wiser. This, of course, was not the only thing he had going on. He was also selling seized weapons that were supposed to be destroyed by the department. He would volunteer to deliver them and doctor the report so no one on the receiving end would know they were missing weapons. A regular entrepreneur he was. Well, he was somewhat caught in a little sting operation that caught him with the goods. Not a really big amount but enough to convict. To spare the department the embarrassment, they fired him and took away his pension instead of a long and public trial that would really make the police force look bad. He would be fired for internal reasons, and that would be the only public knowledge if anyone were to investigate.

Of course, Trevor and his friends do not know the real story, so there is no reason not to do business. Jeremy does have a somewhat big family. He has a white wife and several children of all ages, some in their teens. He is not much of a father to them, unfortunately. They run wild, with their mother working all the time trying to make up for all the losses that Jeremy has caused them. One has got to give her credit for sticking it out with him. He really has no idea how to run a business. His failed business is proof of that. Obviously, he can't even manage his family. Speaks volumes. Trevor is a little nervous about hooking these two up. Jeremy is a friend of a friend of Trevor's.

Jeremy is waiting at the Madhatters for Jason and Trevor, hoping he can make these guys believe his lies so he can get this guy to buy into his company. If Jason puts big money into the business, he will be back on top again. For this to work, he has to put on an award-winning performance.

Great, here they come, Jeremy thinks.

Trevor makes the introductions. "Jeremy, if you don't mind, I am going to let you guys talk. I will be at the bar. Good luck, Jason."

Jeremy spells the whole deal out for Jason, who absolutely loves the plan. They arrange to meet at the office on Monday so Jason can get a real flavor for the business and make his final decision. If this is as good as it looks, then Jason is willing to put lots of money into this deal and really make his one and only dream come true. Jason won a large lawsuit a number of years ago, so he has all the money he needs. He just hopes this is as good as it seems. If it is, he will have everything he has ever wanted. That really excites him, and when he gets excited, he likes to get laid.

Jason thinks to himself, *If this goes well, I am going to have to call Jeanette to celebrate.*

After saying his goodbyes to Jeremy, he goes home all pumped up about how great this deal looks. Trevor left somewhere between "Let's have another drink" and "Let's go check out the office." He will have to call him later and let him know how it went.

"Jeanette? Jason. What are you doing tonight? I would love to take you out," Jason says. "Or stay in," he mutters under his breath.

Jeanette, a lovely figure with a pretty face, has a bit of a past. She was married once, a long time ago. What seems a lifetime ago now? She married a guy that promised her the world and all the money she needed to give her the lifestyle she has always wanted. After a few months, he ended up running off with his secretary. She filed for divorce, and since her sister was a paralegal at a downtown law firm, she was able to get it over pretty quick. She is a little more cautious now, so she doesn't have another failed marriage. Her father always told her that she wants a champagne life on a beer budget. She likes this guy Jason. He is funny and charming and very good-looking and is very satisfying in the area she likes most—in the bedroom. She will hang onto this guy for a while and see where it goes. Jeanette is hoping he has lots of money.

Trevor decides to call his new friend, Christopher, to see what he's doing and if he wanted to get together for some dinner or whatever.

That's weird. He told me he would be home all night, but there is no answer at his house, Trevor thinks to himself, holding the phone in his hand. *Oh well, something probably came up. I'll give him a call later tonight.*

He decides to stop at the store on the way home to get something for dinner tonight. He really did not get anything decent at Madhatters while he was waiting for Jason. He is really hungry now. And he needs to get dog food.

Jason gets to Jeanette's house to pick her up for their date tonight. Jeanette decides to slow it down a little on the sex with him. She doesn't want to blow it this time around, and she is afraid Jason will think that their relationship is all about sex and only about sex. Hopefully, he will understand and slow down a bit too.

Jason takes her to a very nice restaurant that is quiet and easy for them to talk and perhaps get to know each other better. Jason doesn't reveal too much about himself because he thinks it's best to not let Jeanette know that he is quite comfortable in his lifestyle and that he has lots of money. If this relationship goes anywhere, he will tell her in time or just let her know slowly by occasionally buying her gifts and stuff.

Trevor goes to his computer to check his email to see if he got any answers to the ads he ran about wanting some company from men on the internet. He does get one from Christopher that he must have sent last night while he was at work.

Great, he wants to get together sometime this week, Trevor thinks. *He has something he has to tell me, but he can't tell me in an email. Too dangerous. That seems a bit cryptic. I wonder what this is all about. He knows who I work for, so maybe he needs to talk to me about work or something. That's strange that he would send me such an email when we just met. Maybe he's just being silly and wants to have a little mystery in our friendship. Can't really call it a relationship yet. Oh well, I'm sure I will find out in time. Let's see if anyone's on any chat lines tonight.*

Chapter Four

Christopher received an email from Trevor about his cryptic email last night.

"Don't know what's going on but if you wanted to meet somewhere today or tonight, that would be fine. I am somewhat curious about your rather cryptic message." This was all his emails said, so Christopher decides to call him and see if he could come over right away.

He is afraid that if he didn't tell someone what was going on, it could be too late. He has been hearing noises coming from the basement of the second museum for several weeks now, and he finally got the nerve to check it out. The section he was hearing noises from is an area that should have no one working in. It was off-limits, and they were told by their boss, Grant, that that section was closed until further notice, so why were there noises coming from down there?

So Christopher walked down there ever so cautiously. He cannot believe what he's looking at. There are several guys loading what looks like drugs in the shipments that are going to Cairo this month. Grant is there with them.

My God, Christopher thinks, *what's he doing here?* He moves in for a closer look and decides they must be smuggling drugs out of the country.

Those shipments have already passed through customs. He can see the customs sticker on them from where he is sitting.

How is that possible? Christopher wonders. *Once the sticker is on them, they can't be opened again until they arrive at their destination. Who knows how high this goes?*

He has to get out of there before someone sees him, and he has to tell someone, but whom? He knows that Trevor works for some government agency as a computer geek.

But should I tell him? Christopher thinks. *He's going to think I've lost my mind. Damn, and I wanted to have a relationship with this guy.*

Christopher slowly backs out the way he came in and starts running to the next building as soon as he is far enough away. He runs so fast and has never been so scared. Things keep popping into his mind. *Should I call the cops? Who can I trust? What do I do?*

He's almost crying now. He doesn't know what to do. Maybe he should just forget what he saw and just go about his business as if everything is all right. *I don't think I can,* he thinks to himself, so he decides he is going to say something to Trevor. He needs to get out of there and go call him right now.

Then another thought crosses his mind. *What if they have the phones monitored? What if they hear me telling someone about this? Damn… I know, I can send him an email through my phone.*

Christopher grabs his phone and starts nervously typing away.

"Hey, Christopher! You know you're not supposed to be on your phone during work."

Holy shit, it's Grant. "Hey, Grant. What's going on?" Christopher says, hoping that he doesn't sound too nervous. "Sorry, man, just responding to a text from my friend. Wanted to let him know I can't talk to him now… Working!"

"That's okay. Let's see it," says Grant with this grin on his face.

"Oh, just an old friend who's bored at home. Wants to chat. Didn't know I was working. That's all. No biggie," Christopher says as he slips the phone in his pocket, hoping Grant will drop the conversation.

"That's cool. Just don't let me see you with it again," says Grant as he walks away.

Damn, that was close, Christopher thinks to himself. *How did he get there so fast? Did he see me or hear me? He showed up there awful quick. I wonder if he knew I was there. I need to get out of here. I have to finish my email to Trevor. The bathroom—I can go into the bathroom and send it in there. No one will see me in there, and Grant won't be around. Thank God, my shift is almost done. Didn't realize how late it was. Maybe I can meet up with Trevor later and tell him what I saw. He might know who to call or what to do. He must have picked up something being in that place all these years. I sure hope he can help because I don't know where else to turn. I do know this though: I am not coming back here. At least I'm off for the next couple of days. I can figure out what to do. Okay, email sent. Now I need to go back to work and pretend nothing is wrong and get the hell out of here when my shift is over.*

Trevor is now really worried after getting this latest email from Christopher. *Sounds like there is real trouble at the museum,* Trevor thinks. *Hope this isn't some fantasy of his. Don't know him well enough to know whether he is the type to panic at the slightest problem. Well, I guess I can see what it's all about. After all, I really want to get with this guy, so I hope he doesn't turn out to be some freak that is going to go all crazy on me. He suggested in the email to bring Jasmine to the park tomorrow and he will meet me there and explain everything. Oh well, nothing I can do tonight. Need to get some sleep. I have work in the morning.*

Chapter Five

Jason is really getting into this chick Jeanette. She has been so attentive to his every need.

I wonder what she does for work, Jason thinks. *She always changes the subject when I bring it up. Hope it's nothing illegal. Naw, what am I thinking? She is probably just embarrassed by it or something stupid like that. If she doesn't want to talk about it, that's fine by me. I couldn't care less anyway, and besides, if this continues, she will eventually tell me. Right now, we are just having fun, nothing more.*

"Hey, Jeanette," Jason says in the phone after getting her voice mail. "How about getting together tonight?"

Jeanette calls him back almost immediately. "Hey, Jason, I would love to, but I am busy tonight. Can we get together tomorrow night? I just have an appointment tonight."

"Yeah, no problem. I will give you a call sometime tomorrow, and we will figure something out."

I wonder how long I can get away with this, Jeanette thinks.

Jeanette, being a hooker, has clients to satisfy, like Harry, the guy that's coming over tonight. He is one of her regulars, so she doesn't want to disappoint him. Besides, he pays a lot for her services. This should be an interesting conversation with Jason when she finally tells him. That's a conversation she is going to have to put off for as long as possible. She really likes him, and it's the closest she has gotten to a relationship in years. But how do you tell a guy that is really into you that you are a high-priced call girl?

Jason decides to sleep in today and really be lazy. Jeremy is supposed to be calling him sometime this afternoon to discuss the next step in this opportunity of his. They are supposed to be going to his office today to look at the business and give Jason a chance to look at the books and make sure everything is legit. In the meantime, Jason decides to just stay in bed and watch some TV.

Trevor tries one more time to contact Christopher but with very little luck. He decides to take Jasmine for a walk to the park in hopes that maybe he will be there. As they round the corner, Jasmine sees her pal first, Christopher's dog. She almost pulls Trevor's arm out of its socket.

Trevor admits he is pretty happy to see Christopher. And his dog too. *Well, I think Jasmine is more excited to see his dog,* Trevor thinks, *but it's good to see them.*

Trevor and Jasmine approach the dog park fence, and Trevor lets her in the park loose to go play. He walks over to where Christopher is leaning against the fence.

"I have been worried about you, Christopher. You wouldn't call me back or answer the many calls and text messages I left for you."

"Trevor, I am so sorry. I have been so scared these past couple of days, I didn't know what to do."

"Well," says Trevor, "I am here now. What's going on? I assume it has something to do with the museum."

"It does," says Christopher. "You would not believe what I saw."

Christopher tells Trevor all about the men in the lower level of the second museum and that his boss is in the middle of it. He tells Trevor what it looked like and that they shouldn't have even been down there. That alone was suspicious. But the fact that his supervisor was down there right in the thick of whatever that was, it is really not right. If they were doing something illegal like he thought, doesn't it make sense that they—whoever these guys are—would need someone inside to help pull it off?

"Well, I know that whoever this is, they would certainly help whatever this is get into the museum," Trevor says. "Are you sure this isn't just a case of the museum working on a new exhibit, and these men down there are working for your boss getting this exhibit all together for an opening? I mean, why are we jumping to this conclusion when there are so many more logical explanations? At my job, I work on facts. And the facts are really scarce here. I mean, you don't have any idea what this could be or if there is even a hint of illegal activity, do you?"

"No, I guess not," says Christopher. "So how do we get these facts? Something tangible that will at least tell us if there is something going on here that is not really quite right?"

Trevor says, "Well, that's when we start to discreetly investigate what's going on there, if there is something there even. So what you need to do if you want to pursue this is to start discreetly asking questions from supervisors above your boss's pay grade, like casually asking if there are any new exhibits coming. The reason for you asking could be simply that you were looking for some overtime and you know that typically when new exhibits are starting up, there is overtime to be had if you want it."

Christopher says, "That's a great idea. It won't make anyone suspicious."

Jeremy calls Jason and asks him if he would like to come to his office tomorrow for a tour of the office and the books so Jason can see how legit and a good investment the business is. He would really like to sucker this guy into becoming a partner. He is running out of money.

Needs some fresh money to siphon from a new source, Jeremy thinks. *Jason sounds like the perfect patsy.*

"Jason, this is Jeremy. Would you like to come to the office tomorrow and check it out for yourself?"

"Oh, hello, Jeremy," says Jason. "Sure, I would love to come over and see how things run, get a feel for the office, and most importantly, see the books. It's just a matter of routine. I am certain everything is in order."

Yeah, everything is in order all right, Jeremy says to himself. *Just depends which set of books I show you.*

"Great, I will see you in the morning, say 9:00 a.m.?" Jeremy states.

"Perfect. I will see you there," says Jason.

Now that this meeting is set up for Jeremy and Jason, Jason is wondering what he could be doing today. Maybe he will call Trevor and see if he would like to go out for a drink or dinner or something. Then he might need to go shopping for food.

"Trevor, what are you doing tonight? Would you like to go do something? Jeanette has plans tonight, so I can't see her. So I am free as a bird. What do you think?" says Jason.

Trevor responds with "Love to. I could go for some dinner, and drinks are definitely on the menu."

I wonder, Trevor thinks to himself, *if Jeanette told Jason what she does for a living yet. I am betting not. I don't think Jason would be so involved in this relationship this early on if he knew. Well, I cannot tell him. It's up to her to tell him. I introduced them and paid for her first session with Jason. That makes me an accessory to this deceit. But it was Jeanette who decided not to tell him what she is and what she does. That's on her. Of course, somehow I think this is going to come back to bite me in the ass. I just have that feeling.*

Christopher has two more days off until he goes in again on Thursday. Christopher is thinking a lot about what Trevor was saying. *Boy, it does make a certain amount of sense. I really jumped to a huge conclusion without any real facts to go on. Maybe that's why I told him about it so he could straighten me out.*

Chapter Six

It's Thursday, and Christopher is going to work feeling a whole lot better about being there. He walks in with a completely renewed sense of purpose. He still thinks there is something there, but Trevor is right.

Do some checking, and I will find out that everything is fine and there is absolutely nothing to this, Christopher thinks. *God, I am so gay. I'll bet a straight guy wouldn't think there was something wrong where there isn't. Jeez. What Trevor must be thinking. Oh well, I think he still wants to pursue a relationship with me. I hope! I am really hoping this didn't scare him away, thinking I am some lunatic that sees scandal in every corner. Well, I am at work now, so enough of this nonsense.*

Jeremy meets Jason at the front door of the office to greet him with his hand out, ready to completely dupe Jason. He is thinking to himself that he needs to put on one hell of a performance here today if he wants Jason's investment.

"Hello, Jason. Welcome! Let me show you around. Give you a tour and then we can sit down in my office and talk about the books and what makes this company run so well and why we are so happy that you are thinking about joining us."

After the tour, Jason and Jeremy sit down to discuss the finer details of this merger. Jason does really like what he sees and is impressed with this set up and how well it appears to run. He can't help get this nagging feeling in the back of his mind that says this is all too good to be true. One of Trevor's favorite sayings is "If it looks too good to be true, then it probably is."

Although Trevor is the one that brought this opportunity to me, he thinks. *I know he has to have a license with the state. I wonder what they have to say about this company. I need to do some checking before I commit to this. This is a lot of money. Also, I know Jeremy was a cop. In Memphis, I think. I need to see why he is no longer a cop. Is there a story there, or did he just quit the force to start his own company?*

"Jeremy, I do like what I see," Jason says. "I would like to take a few days to mull it over and make a decision. You okay with that? I will call you in a few days, no more than a week."

"Not a problem, Jason," says Jeremy. "Take all the time you need."

Christopher gets to work, and his boss immediately grabs him and takes him aside and tells him that he wants no crap from him tonight. Christopher is confused about what he is talking about. Is he referring to the last time he worked and he found him texting on his phone? This seems excessive for a simple phone violation. Maybe he suspects that Christopher saw more than he was supposed to and that, therefore, there is more to what he suspected than either Christopher or Trevor thought. He appeased him by telling him he won't do it again, but really, that was three days ago, and this seems to be a bit over the top for the offense.

So Christopher gets to work on the project plan for the night. When the employees come in to work, they are given a project plan as to what they are to work on for the night. A project plan can be anything from resetting up a display to be more interesting to the patrons to taking down sets that are being replaced with another. If an employee is on the takedown project, they are rarely on the setup project for the new display.

Grant is one of the leads that sort of runs the crew at night. During his work night and while he is breaking down an out-of-date set, Grant's boss walks in. This is the break he was hoping for. Now he can ask Jonathan about any new displays going on in the second museum, but he has to ask him in a way that he doesn't think it's anything except idle chitchat and curiosity.

Jonathan is Grant's boss. Jonathan does more of what he calls an on-the-cuff job. This means that he is here while the public is here and has to handle things that go wrong during the day—kids messing up the displays or people asking questions of what the display is all about. That sort of thing.

"Hey, Jonathan, how goes the battle?" Christopher says. "Been a while since we saw you on the floor this late at night. Everything okay?"

"Hey, Chris. Yeah, it's been a while since I have seen all of you. Someone has to run the museum when it's open during the day, you know?"

They both laugh, and Christopher says to Jonathan, "Hey, Jonathan, I really prefer Christopher if you wouldn't mind."

"Oh, that's right," Jonathan says. "I forgot. My apologies."

"Quite all right, Jonathan," Christopher says. "Say, Jonathan, I have a question if you wouldn't mind."

It's now or never, Christopher thinks.

"Are there any projects going on in other museums that we aren't aware of? The reason I ask is that I could really use the overtime, and we aren't getting much here. Maybe there is some to be gotten somewhere else?"

"Sorry, Christopher. There are no projects going on in any other museum right now. Just the normal switch out for a new, but none of these are major projects. They can all be completed in one night. Sorry."

Well, that pretty much seals it for Christopher. Jonathan confirmed that there is nothing going on anywhere else in any other museum. So he was right. What to do next? This could be a tough one since he is not the investigator. He has no idea where to go from here. He will talk to Trevor again and see what he thinks about this latest revelation.

Before Christopher has a chance to decide what to do or think about it, Jonathan comes to him when he is working alone and tells Christopher he needs him to come with him right now.

Christopher says, "Why? Where are we going?"

Then Grant comes around the corner, holding a gun, and says, "Wherever I tell you to. You will not say a word, scream, or make any sound at all, or I will put a bullet in your head right now. Let's go!"

Christopher walks in front of them, trying not to make any sudden moves. Jonathan also has a gun now, and they are both pointing them at him. There is not much he can do but comply. So they walk him to the second museum and down to the lower level. As they are walking to the lower level, Christopher trips and falls to the bottom of the stairs. Jonathan and Grant think this was on purpose and they jump down practically on top of him and came really close to shooting him. Christopher has tears running down his cheeks now. He is more scared than he has ever been.

"What are you two doing?" Christopher says. "Why are you doing this? What are you doing down here? What do I have to do with this? You can't really think you can get away with whatever it is you are up to?"

"Shut up, Christopher. Your babbling," Jonathan says.

Grant says, "You realize that when we are done with what we are doing down here, you are history. Dead. We are going to kill you! You will keep quiet and let us do our work. If you behave yourself, we will let you live longer."

Jonathan chimes in, "Grant, why don't we just kill him now and be done with it?"

Grant says, "We may need him to get us out of here, and for that, we need a warm body."

Jonathan says, "To answer your question, Christopher, since we are going to kill you anyway, what we are doing here is a completely automated drug operation. We receive the drugs from overseas through our diplomatic crates, all of which pass through customs. And instead of ending up in the customs lockup, they are sent here and remained unopened until we open them. Since we have been doing this for so long legitimately, it's a matter of normal process, so no one thinks twice about it. Drugs come in, in pure form. We cut them, refine them, and send them out to all parts of the US and even to other parts of the world into waiting drug dealers' hands in museum shipments. Everybody gets rich. One man controls the whole operation as the commander. And when this is all over, you will die!"

Trevor takes Jasmine for a walk and ends up at their favorite doggy park. Unfortunately, Christopher is not there.

Oh well, Trevor thinks. *It's not like we had a date to meet there.*

Although they didn't have plans to meet there, Trevor sends a text message to Christopher to see where he is. After several minutes and no answer, Trevor tries again to see if he is available in the next hour or so. Still no response.

Hmmm, Trevor thinks. *Oh well, maybe he's sleeping or something. After all, the man does work nights.*

Trevor will try again later. In the meantime, he will finish his walk with Jasmine and just stay in for the night.

Christopher is now sitting on the floor in the corner and apparently out of the way of their work. He tries to engage them in conversation, hoping that it won't let them forget he is a person and someone they have known all these years and that it might perhaps be hard to do what they were planning for him. One thing that these two geniuses forgot to do was take Christopher's cell phone away from him. He had it hiding in his left sock. So maybe when they didn't find it on him, they assumed it was in his locker where it was supposed to be. He had to be careful not to raise their suspicion and let them see his cell phone. He managed to send out one text, one word, and only one word: "HELP" in all caps to Trevor.

Trevor is home watching TV with Jasmine at his side. He is watching some show that he was not particularly interested in, wasting time until he goes to bed. He decides to call Jason to see how it went at Jeremy's office.

"Hey, Jason," Trevor says, "I haven't heard from you since you went to his office. How was it? Was it all you thought it would be or what?"

"His operation was pretty impressive," Jason said.

Jason told Trevor all about how it went and what he was looking at as far as checking Jeremy out.

"So, Trevor," Jason says, "how much of this guy's background do you know? Anything you can tell me to fill in the picture a bit? I just want to make sure everything, I mean everything, is on the up and up before I commit."

"Let me see what I can dig up for you," Trevor says. "I don't know as much about him as a friend of mine does so let me see what he has to say. I will let you know in a couple of days, okay? I can tell you that he was a cop in Memphis, and when he left, it was not of his own accord. I don't know much more than that. That's just what I heard. Do not know if it's true or if there is more to this story. But I would check it out before you sign anything or give him a dime. Just my two cents, Jason. After I put you two together, I found out a couple more things that didn't exactly impress me, so tread lightly, okay? Got to go, Jason. Talk to you tomorrow."

Jason says, "Good night, Trevor!"

Trevor gets Christopher's HELP message.

Okay, after the conversation we had, I know he wouldn't send that if there was not something to it now, Trevor thinks. *Okay, now he needs to act and quickly. Let's see, who can I call that can make some discreet inquiries without raising eyebrows? I know this Lieutenant in the Metropolitan Police Department of the District of Columbia, Lt. James Moran, Jimmy to his friends. I can call him and see if there is anything he can do to just see what's going on in there. It might be nothing, or it could be something. Jimmy can find out for me and see if I should raise any red flags. I really hope this is not Christopher being all dramatic over nothing again. I thought I calmed him down and got him to think more clearly about this whole "whatever this thing is."*

"Hey, Jimmy, it's Trevor. How are you? Long time no see. We need to get out and play some ball or something soon. It has been way too long. I think I am getting rusty. Today I am calling for a favor. I wonder if you could look into something for me discreetly. This is what's going on as far as I know."

Chapter Seven

Jeanette calls Jason and asks if there is a plan for them to go out tonight. Jason is not able to go out with her tonight because he is meeting a guy that will hopefully be able to fill in some of the blanks on Jeremy. He has known Jeremy for years and probably knows him better than anyone else. He only has this one opportunity to meet with him, and it has to be tonight because he leaves for Chicago in the morning.

"Hello, is this George Walton?" Jason says into the phone.

"This is George. Can I help you?"

"Hi, George, this is Jason Brandt. I am considering getting into business with Jeremy Blackstone, and I understand you know him and have for a long time. I would appreciate anything you can tell me about him that can help me decide on what to do here. The plan is for me to invest in his security business. It's quite a lot of money, so I am trying to learn as much about the man as I can. Can you help?"

George tells Jason he would be glad to tell him what he knows about Jeremy. He doesn't know as much as he might think. Jeremy likes to keep his personal life pretty close.

"Doesn't like to reveal too much to anyone," George says.

He continues to explain all that he knows to Jason, and Jason thanks him for his information.

He was right. He didn't know all that much about Jeremy. What he did know was why he left the Memphis PD. There was some talk about a drug bust and some missing money and that Jeremy might have been involved in it, but there was no proof, so they let all the parties go instead of pursuing it. So technically they could not prove he had any involvement or not, so there is not a complaint that Jason could look at what was said. Most of that was behind closed doors and not to be revealed to anyone.

From everything else he learned, there was nothing that would spell doom for this investment opportunity. He would invest but over time instead of all at once. Put a certain amount in the pot at first and then give it some time and invest every few months. This way, he can watch things and see if there is anything to be concerned about without putting up everything. So put a contract together that spells out a time line for the investment payments. See if Jeremy will go for that. If he doesn't, then this was not a good deal then because there would be no reason not to go ahead with a plan like this over time unless there was some hanky-panky going on with this offer. This is all he can do for now.

Let's see if Jeanette would like to go out and get a bite to eat and maybe have her for desert, Jason thinks.

"Hey, Jeanette," Jason phones, "are you available to go out tonight? My business finished earlier than I expected. Maybe come over to my house after we get a bite. How does that sound?"

"I would be happy to. Do you want to pick me up?"

"Sure, I will be there in an hour. I thought I would call Trevor and see if he would like to join us for dinner and drinks. Any objections?" says Jason.

"None at all," Jeanette says. "I would love to see him again. Call him."

Trevor is trying to find out anything that can be done to check on the historical museum and to see if there is anything going on there that can explain this HELP message that he got from Christopher. His friend, Lieutenant Jimmy, has told him, "You don't just go barging in to the historical museum with or without a warrant, none of which has been obtained."

So he is not sure what Trevor expects him to do. He has no evidence that a crime was committed. No judge is going to sign off on a warrant without something to go on. There is one thing they could do, and that is make inquiries to the museum discreetly and see if anyone says anything, but this is a big place.

Where do we start looking, and what are we looking for? Trevor thinks.

Trevor's friend is missing, and he would like to help him. But he is not going to put his badge on the line for it. He knows the captain of security that works there, so he will start there and see if his security friend has seen or heard anything. If that proves to be useful, he will go on from there.

"Hey, Rodney. Jimmy here. Do you have time for some coffee later today? Thought I would stop by for a quit chat. I need to talk to you about something, and I need to do it in person."

"Sure," Rodney answers. "Gonna be in the Arinotics Museum at constitution center around three this afternoon. Stop on by."

"Sounds good," Jimmy says, "See you around four or so, and thanks."

Trevor has been worried about Christopher, but there is nothing he can do right now, at least until Jimmy can check it out. He says he will help, but if there isn't anything concrete or if no one saw anything out of the ordinary going on there, it's going to be hard to keep Jimmy interested enough to keep looking.

I can't see Christopher sending out a one-word help message if there wasn't something to this. I just hope he's all right, Trevor keeps thinking to himself.

He's driving himself crazy not knowing what's going on. Well, he will hear from Jimmy later, and it will either be something or not. *Time to get something to eat and feed Jasmine,* he thinks.

Jimmy arrives at the historical museum to chat with his friend.

"Rodney, how the heck are you? Long time no see."

Rodney greets his old friend by shaking his hand.

"So here is what I have heard and it's from an employee that works here."

Rodney asks, "Who is this employee?"

"I would rather not say at this time since we don't really have any hard evidence right now."

Jimmy explains to Rodney what Trevor had told him about the goings-on in the lower level.

Jimmy asks, "So have you heard or have you been told of any activity on the lower levels, like in the setup area or the shipping areas? They are all on that same lower level, right? It's been a while since I have been here. Well, is there any reason we can't go down and check it out right now?"

Rodney replies, "Sure. I saw some workers down there a few days ago, but what's weird maybe is that I have not seen anyone down there in the last couple of days. Here, it's this way."

Rodney leads Jimmy down a corridor toward this huge elevator. They take this elevator to the lower level, which is one level below the floor they are on. The setup room is where they build their displays for the museum. This huge elevator is how they get those bigger displays up to their final spot on the museum floors. Not far from this room is the dock area where everything comes in.

"Okay," Rodney says, "this is it."

They walk into this huge room that has several projects in partial setup stages. They decide to split the room up and see if they see anything odd or out of place. Neither one of them are sure what it is they are looking for. Jimmy, being a seasoned cop, is certain that if there was anything out of the ordinary, he would see it, at least he hopes so.

Trevor wasn't sure what it was that we should be investigating, or if there is anything even to investigate. Jimmy figured that since he has a friend inside, he will just bluff his way inside and hope for the best.

Trevor rarely gets this way, so he has learned over time to take it seriously that if he thinks something is wrong, it probably is. Trevor has really a good grasp on things and gets these feelings that even he can't explain.

They turn on all the lights and start searching for whatever it is they are looking for. Jimmy searches over to the right and Rodney over to the left, more toward the huge dock door that separated the setup room from the loading dock.

"Here. Over here, Rodney."

Oh my god, Jimmy thinks, *Trevor was right. Son of a bitch, there's a body over here. Christ, he has been beaten badly and then stabbed in the back for his trouble.*

Jimmy turns him over and asks Rodney, "Do you know this guy?"

Rodney replies, "Nope, never seen him before. Does he have a wallet or an ID to the museum?"

"Let me see. Checking his pockets."

While Jimmy is checking all his pockets, Rodney starts looking around to see if there is anything around that someone might have used, like a tool or wrench or something that could have done this amount of damage to this poor guy.

"I know this guy. He is this Christopher fellow that works upstairs. I just found his museum ID badge." Jimmy spouts out that he found a wallet in this guy's coat pocket.

"Oh boy!" Jimmy exclaims. "This guy's name is Christopher Jenkins. Lives in the west village."

Looking in his wallet for other IDs of some sort, Jimmy didn't find anything really helpful other than a picture of this great-looking dog. But really nothing that would tell him anything other than who he was. His driver's license pretty much told them that.

I think this is the guy Trevor was worried about, Jimmy thinks. *I am certain he said his name was Christopher.*

"Well, this is now a police investigation. We need to not touch anything else," Jimmy says.

Rodney says, "I will lock this room down so no one can get in here until your forensic people arrive. Have them check in with me at the front desk, and I will escort them down here. It's hard to find if you don't know this place."

"Thanks, Rodney. Now I have to go and tell a very good friend that his friend is dead."

Chapter Eight

Jeanette goes and runs a hot bath for her to get ready for her date with Jason. Jason, in the meantime, calls Trevor to see if he would like to join them for dinner and some drinks. It's been a while since they were together, and it would be a great time to catch up.

As the phone rings, Trevor is putting some dog treats into his favorite girl's food as a special surprise for her.

"Hello."

"Trevor, it's Jason. Jeanette and I are going out to the plastic burger house for dinner and drinks and wanted to know if you would like to join us. Nothing special, just a casual evening with friends."

"Jason, that sounds great, but I am busy tonight," Trevor says. "Any other night and it's a go."

"Sounds good, buddy. Let me know when you aren't busy, and I will tell you the latest about this business deal with Jeremy."

"You got it. Have one on me. Talk soon."

Jimmy arrives at Trevor's house to give him the bad news. A doorbell rings, and Trevor answers alongside his favorite pooch, Jasmine. She loves greeting visitors at the front door.

"Hey, Jimmy," Trevor says as he opens the door.

"I thought I would stop by and give you an update from my visit to the historical museum," Jimmy says. "Trevor, what was the name of that guy you were telling me about? Chris or Christopher, wasn't it something like that?"

"Yeah, he liked to be addressed as Christopher."

"Do you know his last name by chance?" Jimmy asks.

"I don't. You see, we just met. We had our dogs in common. I met him at the dog park down the road. He and I would sit and watch our dogs play. We went out a few times, and I met him at the historical museum a couple of times. I never bothered to ask for his last name. It never even occurred to me. I suppose I would have eventually if we had spent more time together. Jimmy, you're scaring me a little here. Why all the questions about Christopher? What did you find at the museum?"

Jimmy was kind of in deep thought, trying to figure the best way to tell him that Christopher is dead and to tell him how he died.

"Trevor, I know this might come as a shock, but your friend is dead. He was beaten to death and then stabbed in the back after all that. Someone really wanted to make sure he was dead. We just opened an investigation into what happened there. My friend at the museum and I found him in the setup area of the lower levels. I looked in his wallet, and his name was Christopher Matthew Jenkins. He was thirty-eight and had a beautiful picture of his dog in his wallet. Not much else, I'm afraid. Trevor, who at this moment has his head in his hands is not freaking out but is starting to hyperventilate and is not saying a word."

He was really hoping for a good long relationship with this guy. He really liked him.

"I wish you would say something, Trevor. I am really sorry about your friend. I know you weren't that close yet, but I have known you for many years and I know that this would have been a relationship had you known him longer. For that, I am also very sorry about. Is there anything I can do for you?"

Trevor lifts his head up and says, "Yeah, actually there is something you can do. Let me investigate this with you."

"Trevor, you know I can't do that. This is a police investigation. I can't bring in a civilian to help with an investigation. My bosses would kill me and then fire me for that."

"You know I can do this, Jimmy. Look what I do for work. I spend my day investigating government agencies and all the crap that goes with that. I can do this. Let me help, please? I beg of you."

"My friend, you're killing me here," says Jimmy.

After sitting there saying nothing for what seemed to Trevor an eternity, Jimmy finally says reluctantly, "Okay, I will let you tag along, but—and hear this good, Trevor—I am the cop here. You follow my lead and do what I say, and if my bosses get wind of anything, we stop immediately. I cannot lose my badge over this."

"You got it. I will not get in your way, but I can help with this whole thing. It's the least I can do for my friend—find out who did this to him. Thanks, Jimmy."

"I hope I am not shooting myself in the foot over this, but I do understand why you want to help—to honor your friend. Okay, I will go back to the station and see where we are at on this so far. I *am* the investigator on this. I requested it as soon as we found him. My captain didn't even hesitate. Since I found the body, he said it was mine to pursue. So at least we have that for now."

"Okay, so what's our first move?"

"Well, we go back to the scene of the crime, talk to the employees that work in that area, and see if anyone can shed some light on why he was down there and if they know what was really going on in the setup area or the loading dock. My gut says no one is going to know anything even if they really do."

"So they will clam up because you are a cop and no one likes to talk to the police," says Trevor.

"Now you're catching on. I think we need to know why Christopher was even down there. According to what Rodney told me, he doesn't work in that area or anywhere near there. He works with the displays after they get up to their display location. He had no reason to be down there. Just so you know, my friend didn't recognize him by his face, but he looked up his name on their computer to see if he did in fact work there, and he does. That's how he found out where in the building he works. Well, I have to go and get this started. I will call you later."

"Thanks, Jimmy. I appreciate you sticking your neck out for me on this."

"No worries. Just don't make me regret it. Talk to you soon."

Jason goes over to Jeanette's to pick her up. When he gets to the door, he gives her a big hug and a very passionate kiss before saying, "Wow, you smell great, and you look great. I am a really lucky guy."

"Shall we go?"

Jason has this worried look on his face that he can't hide from Jeanette.

"Okay, so what's going on?" she asks.

"What makes you think there is anything going on?" Jason remarks.

"I know that look? You are worried about something. I can feel it. So tell me. What has you frowning?"

"Well, when I called Trevor to join us, he said he was busy, but I sensed it in his voice. He was really upset about something. Would you mind if we dropped by to see him and find out what's going on?"

"Absolutely," she answers. "We can have dinner anytime. Let's go see what's up with him."

A ring of the doorbell a few minutes later and Trevor opens the door to greet with some surprise that Jason and Jeanette were there.

"Thought you were going out to dinner? Why are you here?"

Jason speaks up, saying, "I was worried about you, buddy. You didn't sound so good on the phone earlier. So what's going on? And don't tell me nothing."

"You two don't want to hear about all of this. You should just go out to dinner like you planned." Trevor tries to end this conversation before it starts.

"Look, something is going on, and I know it. Now we are not leaving until you tell us what this is about. So start talking."

"Fine, I didn't want to bother anyone else about this, but since you are insisting, I will tell you what I know. Remember I told you about this guy I met at the dog park? He was a great guy and has a beautiful dog that Jasmine is quite fond of. Jasmine and his dog would run and roll around and just play together. It was really great for her. His name is Christopher. You know how hard it is for me to make friends. Well, I felt we had a connection through our dogs. So we started talking and having a great conversation, and I really connected with him. Someone I can talk to about pretty much anything."

"Isn't that what I have always been there for? To be your friend and help you out? That's what friends are for, right?" Jason tries to put their own friendship into perspective.

"I know, and I appreciate you always being there for me."

"We have always been there for each other," Jason fires back.

"When I met Christopher, it was just really cool to have another good friend," says Trevor.

So Trevor tells Jason and Jeanette what happened. Jason is listening intently, and one could see that he felt really bad for his friend.

"Oh my god, Trevor. I can't believe any of this. He was murdered in the basement of the historical museum. Beaten. Who would do such a thing? Do the police have any leads? That friend of yours, Lieutenant Jimmy something—does he have any idea who or why this happened?"

"Not yet," Trevor says. "But the investigation just started. They aren't even sure when this happened. Jimmy and the head of security for the museum just found him this morning. So this security friend of Jimmy's locked up the setup room and waited for the forensic team to get there. That's all I know at this point. Jimmy found his wallet, so that's how he knew who he was and where in the museum he worked. I did get him to promise to keep me in the loop on things."

Trevor didn't want to tell Jason that he actually made Jimmy promise to let him work the investigation with him. He didn't want Jason to be worried about him. He was always kind of protective of him ever since they met. It was actually kind of sweet, but in this case, the less Jason knew, the less grief he would get.

Jimmy gets back to the station and sits down to see if any of the reports are there for this murder. Not a minute goes by, and the head of the forensic team comes charging in straight to Lieutenant Jimmy's desk.

"Jimmy, what the hell, man?"

"What do you mean 'What the hell'? Where are my reports on the museum murder? You know the one—historical museum… murder…reports? Feel free to chime in here."

"That's just it, Jimmy. What murder? We get to the museum, and this guy Rodney escorts us down to where this alleged murder was to happen. No body, no evidence there even was a murder."

Jimmy jumps up throwing this forensic guy practically off his feet. "What do you mean there is no body?" Jimmy shouts for everyone to hear.

"That's what I am telling you. There was no body for us to examine or retrieve back to autopsy. Nothing."

"Well, what did Rodney say when you discovered no body? He was with me when we found him."

"He told us that the two of you were down there and discovered a body, as well as discovered who he was. He was just as surprised as I was to not find the body. So we searched the rest of the room and the dock area. No body anywhere. So we came back here."

"Kind of hoping you had something to add to this."

"If he was truly dead, it has been my experience they do not get up and walk out."

Jimmy caught his sarcasm. His mind was going superfast trying to figure out what is going on here.

How the hell do I tell Trevor we lost his friend's body? he thinks to himself. *Well, first order of business is going back to have a little chat with one Rodney. I think this had better be without Trevor since I don't know how to tell him of this latest development. I will let him get some sleep, and we will pick this up in the morning.*

Jimmy races out the door to get his patrol car. He speeds over to the historical museum to talk to Rodney.

I hope he has answers for me.

This is the weirdest case so far that he has had in a long while. He has this nagging feeling this one is going to end up being personal.

He finally arrives at the museum and to the front door. He stops to ring the overnight bell. It's now after closing, and the night shift is on. The doors are locked, so you have to be buzzed in. Good thing he called Rodney to let him know he was coming. Rodney would have been gone thirty minutes ago if he hadn't. Rodney actually buzzes him in and then rises to greet his friend.

"I know what you are going to say. I don't know what happened myself. I locked up the room and turned off the badge sensors so no one would be able to get in. The next time I entered was to escort your forensic people down here. That's when we discovered the body had been removed from here. I can't explain it. No one should have been able to get in here."

Jimmy wasn't blaming Rodney. He has known him for a very long time.

It is strange though, Jimmy thinks to himself. *He says no one was able to get in here. I believe him. As any good detective will tell you, you have to look at the facts in front of you and then decide what to do. Who is lying to you? Who is telling the truth? What is the truth?*

Jimmy determines his next steps by running everything he knows presently through his mind and then sifting through it and see what logic says he should do.

"Take me to your setup room, Rodney. I want to see the whole room, as well as the dock area."

Rodney points his hand down the same corridor as before, and they head back to the setup area as they did yesterday. This time, however, Jimmy tells Rodney he wants to walk down the stairs and check out the security door at the bottom of the stairs.

"So when you lock all the badged doors out, that includes this one?" Jimmy asks.

"Correct. I just locked off all doors leading to this level of the museum. That includes anything from the dock area to this room and everything from this room to the loading docks."

As they approach the door at the bottom of these stairs, Rodney takes out his security badge and unlocks the door so they can enter. One thing Jimmy does is stop and scan the room. Trying to see from a whole visual of this room will tell him. Then he walks over to the area where they discovered the body.

"So as far as you know, no one has been down here since you and I left here?" Jimmy rechecks his facts with his friend.

"Nope, no one has been down here," says Rodney.

"So how do you explain that the body we found was gone before our forensic people got here? We are talking about perhaps an hour, maybe less."

Jimmy is really confused about how this body got out of here in less than an hour.

"Well, there are two possibilities," Jimmy explains. "One, someone was able to bypass your security, or it wasn't as secure as you say it was, or someone was already down here when we were and remained hidden until we left and then somehow got a body out of here in under an hour."

"Any thoughts?" Jimmy asks Rodney.

"Well, I can tell you that when this security is locked down, all indications on our boards upstairs show they were in lockdown. The boards will show that on the security tapes, which I can show you. We have them saved on tape for seven days."

"So assuming that's right, and I will want to see those tapes, then someone was down here hiding while we were here."

"That is a little unsettling, don't you think?" says Rodney.

Well, Jimmy couldn't think what else it could be, so he told Rodney to start looking for places someone could hide and be completely quiet when they were here. Jimmy is thinking loading dock.

"Someone had to be in there while we were down here. We would have seen someone else if they were in here. I am certain of it."

So after checking out the loading dock, there was really nothing more for them to see here. It was time to leave and start investigating elsewhere. He has to go talk to Trevor and let him know this latest piece of information that he is not going to like.

Chapter Nine

Jimmy is meeting with the forensic guy at the historical museum where the murder took place.

"Okay, so what time exactly did you get to the museum?" Jimmy asks the head of the forensic team.

"Exactly twenty minutes after you called it in, 7:22 p.m."

"Okay, so that gives us a twenty-minute window in which someone was able to expertly remove that body and leave no evidence that it was even there. Did you run a scan to see if there was any blood on the floor or on the furniture?"

"I did, and we found a very small amount of blood on the bench this body was supposed to be under. There was nothing anywhere else in the area where you found the body. And for the moment, I will assume there was a body for the sake of conversation, and I know you. If you say there was a body, there was a body."

"Well, thank you for that. So we need to figure out how a body was removed in twenty minutes without a trace and how there was practically no forensic evidence. Okay, so we know someone had to be down here while we were here. It's not unreasonable to assume this person was hiding somewhere in this room or the loading dock. This room looks to be pretty open. I don't see any places to hide where we would not see them."

Jimmy walks around the room and checks under cabinets, desks, and any place a person could hide. There is no place a normal-sized person could hide in this room without Rodney and Jimmy seeing them. The loading dock is a completely different case though. There are a lot of places for someone to hide in there. But the thing is, they didn't go out to the loading dock.

Maybe that was the plan from the start, Jimmy thinks. *Put the body there, so we will see it right away. That would probably stop us from going to the dock or anywhere else. The body had to be moved there after he was dead. Forensics did not find much blood at all. So he definitely was not beaten and stabbed here.*

As Jimmy walks out to the loading dock, Rodney asks, "Hey, Jimmy, what do think you will find out there? We never went out there."

Rodney seems a little nervous now, Jimmy thinks. *I think he thinks that this issue will not look good for him. A body discovered and lost on his watch. His boss is not going to like this, and Rodney could possibly lose his job over this.*

"I am going out here to see if I can find some evidence that someone was here recently like when we were here last," Jimmy says.

Jimmy proceeds out to the loading dock. There are two large doors in this area, and one of them is not closed all the way at the bottom. That could be nothing, but it certainly could be something too. He turns back to Rodney and asks him about this.

Rodney replies, "Well, the doors have an alarm on them. If they are not closed all the way up to about a one-inch gap, the alarms would sound, so the door can be not closed at the floor an inch and that would not trigger my alarms."

"So let me see if I got this right," Jimmy says. "If the doors are not closed to about an inch from the floor, the alarms would sound. So if someone dragged this body out of here through here, that would sound the alarms, right?"

"Yes, that's right," states Rodney with some authority now.

"Okay, so can we assume then that the body did not get out of here this way?" Jimmy asks.

"That would be a reasonable assumption," Rodney says.

"Okay, I have seen enough," says Jimmy. "Let's go."

This is really going to bug me, Jimmy thinks to himself. *I can't see how they got him out of here then. Something just doesn't wash here.*

"Rodney, I need you to show me one more thing before I leave. Show me your alarm panel upstairs, the one you monitor."

Rodney escorts Jimmy upstairs to look at the panel on the monitoring station they keep monitored 24-7.

"Okay, so explain these lights and gadgets here." Jimmy is now pointing to the station that has all these camera lights lighting up all over the place and buttons that their guards are pushing. "Show me the monitor of the dock doors and the alarm that would go off with the doors partially up."

Rodney explains all the buttons and alarms and then shows him the cameras in the dock area, as well as the setup room. "What I can tell you is that not much is seen on these cameras in off-hours because the rooms are usually dark with lights out after the last person leaves for the day."

"Okay, so if the doors are open just an inch and the alarms don't go off, why can't we see the daylight under that door?"

"The only thing that comes to mind is that when we were down there, it was already starting to get dark outside," Rodney tries to explain this to Jimmy. "That along with the fact that the dock has a very long driveway that leads up to these doors. It's unlikely that we would see any light once it starts getting dark."

"Okay, I think I understand now how things work." Jimmy looks back at Rodney and takes his leave of him to go do some investigating on his own.

Rodney still seems a bit nervous during all this, Jimmy thinks. *I wonder why.*

"Jason, I really don't know much after that, but Jimmy promised to keep me up to speed on his investigation so I should know more tomorrow morning," Trevor explains.

"I am surprised you didn't ask him to let you tag along."

"Well, this is a murder investigation. He would have said no, and we both know it. Why put the man on the spot?"

"So there is plenty of time to go out to eat still. Why don't we all go out?"

"I am doing nothing except sitting here wondering. I could use the distraction," Trevor says, desperately trying to change the subject so Jason doesn't start quizzing him about more on this.

He always has to know more and more even if there isn't any, Trevor thinks. *I love Jason, but sometimes he can be a real pain.*

"Jeanette, what do you think? Want to go to eat still, or did you want to call it a night? Your call."

"I am okay with going out to eat still if Trevor goes with us."

"Yeah, I'm in," Trevor says.

"Okay, then let's go," states Jeanette.

They leave Trevor's place after he puts Jasmine out and lets her do her business before they go. Once he lets her back in, they leave in Jason's car.

They have a very nice time at this favorite restaurant of theirs. The owners come over and greet them. After coming here for years as regulars, they have made many friends here. That's why Jason likes coming here. Friends are stopping by their table all night greeting them. Madhatter is a great place to unwind.

They order their food, and once it comes, Trevor eats a little but tells Jason and Jeanette that he is not all that hungry, so they engage in some idle chitchat while he picks at his food.

Jason finally opens up the conversation. "Trevor, Jimmy is good. He will find out what happened. Don't worry. Besides, it's not like you knew Christopher that long. Come on, how many times did you go out? Once, twice?"

Now Trevor is getting pissed. *Typical Jason,* he thinks.

"It doesn't matter how many times we saw each other. He was my friend. Don't you dare treat that as trivial. Plus the man died. No, he was murdered. That means something, and if you don't like it, then fuck you!"

"Look, Trevor. I certainly didn't mean for you to think I was taking this tragedy as trivial. I just meant that since you haven't known him long, there are probably a lot of things you don't know about him. That's all."

Jason did some major back stepping to apologize in his own way to Trevor. He doesn't like to see him like this.

I just hope this isn't going to become a big thing for Trevor, Jason thinks. *He gets wrapped up in these things because he is just so sensitive about some things. I can't quite put my finger on it, but Trevor always seems to get this way on things that matter the most to him.*

"Well, let's just talk about something different, huh? Don't you have to be getting back to work soon?"

"I do. Tomorrow! I only took a couple of days off so I can help Christopher. I have to just be patient and see what Jimmy comes up with."

"Okay. Jeanette, you done?" asks Jason.

"Yeah, good to go."

"Okay, let's get out of here," Trevor says.

As they approach Trevor's house, Trevor asks loudly, "Isn't that Jimmy in an unmarked police car?"

"Yeah, I think it is. Seems he is probably waiting for you," Jason states.

They pull into the driveway, and Trevor hops out before Jason even stops the car. Running to Jimmy's car, Trevor stops in the middle of the street as Jimmy walks toward him.

"So what have you found so far?"

Jimmy tells Trevor, "Maybe we should go inside."

"Jimmy, you remember Jason?"

"I do. Hello, Jason. Been a while."

Jason responds back in kind. "So, what have you found out about Trevor's friend?"

"Let's go inside," Jimmy says as he ushers them into the now open front door. "There has been a development. Trevor, I am so sorry, but something weird happened. When our forensic team got to the museum—and we are talking twenty minutes tops—they went down to the setup room, and Christopher's body was gone."

"Wait, what? His body was gone? How is that even possible? Dead bodies don't just get up and walk out. Where did it go? Was he really dead when you checked him? Maybe he really isn't dead." Trevor is starting to get excited and not in a good way.

"Okay, Trevor, just stop a minute and take a breath. We don't know what happened yet. We are working on the alleged crime scene.

And yes, he was very dead when I examined him at the crime scene. We are not even sure the museum or at least the setup room is the actual crime scene. We have our doubts because there was very little blood there and very little forensic evidence. That's like DNA, evidence of a fight, or the kind of beating he took. If it happened there where we found him, there would be a lot more blood, evidence of that kind of crime. And there simply was not and not by a long shot. He was beaten and murdered somewhere else and moved to where we found him.

"Now my initial thoughts on this was that he was in the process of being moved when we discovered his body. I think that they were hiding somewhere else like in the dock area, waiting for us to leave. What I think is that there was already something in the works to move him, and we interrupted them from what they were doing. They left the body where it was and ran and found a place to hide. We only searched the area where the body was found. We didn't go into the dock area to clear it. They could have been outside the dock doors. We found one of the doors not closed all the way to the floor.

"We are investigating this, and I know I said I would let you help, but I think the best thing for you to do, Trevor, is go back to work tomorrow. And if I need anything like online help or searching for clues over the wires, I will call you, okay?"

Jason is now giving Trevor that "I don't like this look" that Trevor knows so well. It's when someone lied to him, or doesn't exactly tell the whole truth. Jason hates liars.

"So he was just going to keep you informed, was he? You lied to me about your involvement in this. He agreed to let you assist in the investigation? Not what you told me."

"Well, Jason," Jimmy states, "if it puts your mind at ease, due to these new developments, I can't let him assist. This, whatever this is, could get ugly real fast, and I would most definitely lose my badge if I let Trevor help. Sorry, Trevor, but that's the way it has to be. I will keep you informed as best I can about ongoing stuff, but you need to sit on the sidelines for this."

"No, I understand. Besides, I have to get back to work tomorrow. That will keep me busy and out of your hair." Trevor says begrudgingly. "I do want to be kept in the loop though. Please?"

Chapter Ten

Trevor returns to work to start decrypting intelligence documents that the FBI brings in.

Looks like there is a deadline, he thinks to himself.

This should be enough for him to keep distracted while Jimmy does his thing. Trevor has several programs that he runs in order to do this. As he is running one of the more complicated programs, his boss walks over, just beaming about something. He looks like the cat that ate the canary.

As he gets closer, Trevor sits back in his chair and says, "You look like you have something good to say, Mark."

Mark Thomas has been his boss for most of his career there. He really likes him, and he has been very good about trying to get him into new things that will advance his career. He has been with this agency for over thirty years and knows everyone that has come and gone over those years and yields a great deal of respect in this—for lack of a better term—spy community.

"I have great news for you," Mark says. "I have been talking with some of the boys in the FBI minor crimes unit, and they tell me they are looking for a fresh candidate to start training for a position with that team. I gave them your name, and they promised me they would give you a look-see. That would put you on the path to where you have always wanted to be: in the spy game. Although they really don't call it that anymore, it might get your foot in the door. Let me know if there is anything I can do to help you."

"Wow, sir," Trevor says, shaking his hand vigorously, "that's awesome. Thanks for getting them to look. I will do the best I can to make a great impression. Thank you so much."

"I know you will. Good luck."

This bit of news got Trevor thinking even more about Christopher and this investigation. He thinks to himself, *I could be even more of a help to Jimmy with this in my background. Okay, Trevor, stop this. You are doing exactly what Jason was saying. I start getting way ahead of myself, and half the time, it doesn't even pan out. I will stop and wait to see if they reach out and want to talk to me. Jeez. Trevor! I do know that I will not jinx this by telling Jason about this. Besides, if I get this, I know there will be some intense training. So we are just letting this bit of news go for now. Concentrate on what I am doing right now, and that is decrypting these documents.*

This process takes Trevor most of the day, but in that time, he has decrypted over twenty documents. It was a good day.

Time to head for home and sit in my house and contemplate what is going on with Jimmy's investigation. Hey, I know, he practically says it out loud for everyone to hear as he exits the building. I will take Jasmine for a walk to the dog park. Who knows? I might see Christopher there. Son of a bitch, there I go again.

"Trevor," he says to himself, "Christopher is dead. He will not be at the dog park."

Jason arrives at Jeanette's house to take her to dinner. They have been going out for a long time now, and it's time they started to get a bit more serious, at least that is what Jason is thinking. He will ask her how she feels about him tonight, opening up the conversation so he can tell her how he feels.

The doorbell rings.

"Be right there!" Jeanette yells to the door.

She finishes up getting ready, which only takes a few seconds as she rushes to the front door. When she opens it, Jason is standing their grinning cheek to cheek, holding a bouquet of roses.

"You look beautiful, Jeanette. I got these for you."

"Wow, that is so sweet of you. Come in. Let me put these in water, and then we can go. I am all ready."

Jason decides, *We are not going to our normal spot tonight.*

He thinks of some place special with a great romantic ambience and light music playing in the background. He is thinking Taberna del Alabardero, which is one of the most romantic restaurants in the DC area.

Great food, I've heard. Never been there, but tonight might just be the right time to check it out.

"Okay, I am ready to go. Miss me? You were somewhere else just now. Want to tell me where?"

"No, it's stupid. Let's just go," Jason says while ushering Jeanette out the door. He was thinking that he wanted to propose to Jeanette because he really does love her.

Love has never really come easy for him. It has always been just lust, only lust without feelings. Now he has these feelings he wants to share with her. He always wants to be with her. He hopes she feels the same way. He cares very deeply about her and all that is about her.

If that isn't love, then I don't know what it is, Jason thinks.

"So, Jeanette, I thought we would go somewhere new tonight, Taberna del Alabardero," Jason tells her. "I hear the food is great and the ambiance is really more toward romantic than what we have gone to before, so I have been told."

Once they arrive at the restaurant and are seated, Jeanette asks Jason, "Where did you find this place? This is great. I hope the food is as good as their reviews, well, the ones you have heard of anyway."

"How about some wine? Or, I know, champagne. How about that?"

"That sounds great. Are we celebrating something?" Jeanette asks.

"Just to be here with you and how happy you make me," Jason responds back. "That's all. I just wanted to tell you how much you mean to me and how proud I am to have you on my arm, so to speak. Can I ask if you feel the same way? Or how do you feel about us? I don't want this to feel weird or anything."

"Jason, I adore you. I love you so much. I have never felt this way about someone before. I know what you are thinking, but not yet. Let's wait a while. When the time is right, I will say yes. It's just not right today but soon."

Jeanette is thinking that she needs to reach out and talk to Trevor.

I know Jason was going to ask me to marry him, Jeanette thinks to herself. *I know he does not know what I do for a living, and I need to know what Trevor thinks we should do before I accept. I hated putting Jason off like that, but I can't without talking to Trevor. This could be ugly if Jason doesn't approve of what I do, and I am certain he won't.*

"Why don't we just finish our dinner?" Jeanette says. "Tonight could you just drop me off? I have an early day tomorrow."

"Yeah, not a problem," Jason says.

As they approach Jeanette's door, she could see that since she told him to wait, he has been really quiet. Jeanette stops him at the bottom of the stairs.

"Jason, you have been really quiet. I didn't say no. I just said wait. I am sorry if that isn't what you wanted to hear. You didn't actually ask me."

"But you know I was going to," Jason says.

"I just didn't want to rush this. I really do love you, and I do want to marry you. The time is just not right, now. But it will be. I promise."

"Was it just a coincidence that tonight you didn't want to stay the night? You have never done that before."

"I really do have an early morning tomorrow. I have clients coming in from out of town, and they will only be here part of the day. I just wanted to be fresh and prepared for tomorrow's meeting. That's all. I promise."

"I get it," Jason says. Sorry I was being a downer. Truth is, I have a pretty early one myself tomorrow. I am meeting Jeremy at his office to go over paperwork. We were supposed to meet there at 7:00 a.m. His office is in Garrett Park, which is not real close to me, so I have to get up early to get there with traffic."

Giving her a long passionate kiss, he says in a real soft sweet voice, "So you are off the hook for tonight."

He gives her one more kiss and says his goodbyes.

Jeanette pulls out her phone the second she closes the door behind her. To Trevor she texts, "Do you have a minute to talk?"

She is hoping he is okay with a phone call tonight. After about ten minutes or so, she hears the ringing of her phone for text messages. She has a different sound for the text messages, so without looking, she knows whether it's a phone call or a text message. It's Jason telling her good night one last time.

What a sweetheart. I am definitely going to marry that man someday. She is thinking all this while responding to his message. It seems a second or two later when Trevor responds to her message.

He says, "I am driving home from the office. I will call you when I get home, okay?"

Jeanette responds back, telling Trevor that would be fine. Jeanette is a little apprehensive about what to tell Trevor since he was the one who fixed them up in the first place.

Correction, he didn't fix us up, Jeanette thinks. *He paid me to fuck Jason, period. Talk about going off the rails. Maybe it is my task to carry out instead of Trevor. Well, I will see what he says, and we will go from there. One thing is sure, Trevor will be pissed over this, especially if he loses Jason as a friend. Dammit, what have I done?*

Jeanette grabs the phone as it starts to ring. "Hello, Trevor, thanks for calling me. I have to tell you something, and I need you to not be driving when I do. Tonight, Jason and I went to this really nice restaurant. Trevor, I know he was going to ask me to marry him."

"Wait, what!" Trevor yells into the phone. "And you said what?"

"I told him—before he asked—to wait," Jeanette says. "I told him, 'I know what you are going to ask me, and I want to, but please wait."

"Are you out of your frickin' mind, lady?" Trevor is now yelling loudly into the phone. "I paid for you to have sex with him. ONCE! what the hell are you doing? And now he wants to marry you? Tell me, did you by *any* chance tell him what it is you do for a living, huh?"

"Well, the subject really never came up more than a couple of times."

"And what did you say?" Trevor is now obviously pissed as he tries to calm down and figure out what to do next.

"Well, I just told him I was in the customer service industry, and I worked for a company that spends the day talking to customers about what they need."

"Oh great. So he has no idea you are a high-priced hooker. And when did you plan to tell him of your actual career path?" Trevor says really sarcastically.

"Well, I was kind of hoping you would tell him," Jeanette again says really quietly.

"Oh boy. Really? And I would do that because why?"

"Well, it was you who introduced us, and Jason is going to remember that, don't you think?"

Jeanette is really trying to be so sweet about this because she knows what position she is putting him into. Jason is his best friend, and either way this is going to hurt someone.

As Jeanette thinks about all the points why they shouldn't tell him or why it shouldn't be her, Trevor pipes up and says, "Okay, I don't see any way out of this for either of us, so I will tell him but in my own way. Are you still hooking, or did you give it up for Jason?"

"I am doing it on a half-time basis. I only see special longtime customers. I stopped all the rest."

"I thought you two were just having some laughs together. I had no idea it was getting this serious," Trevor says a little calmer. "Okay, I will handle it. When you say you asked him to wait, what exactly does that mean? Are you going to tell him when he can ask you or is he just going to pick another time?"

"We didn't really discuss that, but I assume he will ask me down the road a bit. I did tell him that I wanted to marry him too, just not now, so I'm not sure when he will ask again."

"Okay, just do what you want to do, and I will figure out the best time to let him know. But if you *are* serious about marrying him, you have to stop hooking even your special clients. Are you hearing me?"

"Yes, yes. I will tell them the next time I see them I will no longer be able to be with them."

"All right, and I will tell Jason in my own time. So leave that to me, okay?" Trevor says to Jeanette.

Jeez, talk about putting me in the middle of a disaster waiting to happen, Trevor thinks to himself. *I can't imagine how Jason is going to take this regardless of when I tell him.*

Trevor is now thinking he should have stopped this way back when they started spending more time together.

I should have told him then that she was a hooker, and he probably would never have gotten this serious with her. Son of a bitch, it's as much my fault as hers... but more of hers. Well, there is no sense placing blame. We now have to deal with it. She obviously loves him, and he definitely loves her. So we will have to plan for a wedding here in the near future. I have not talked to Jason in a while. Maybe I should call him just to check in and tell him about the latest on Jimmy's investigation. Sort of an excuse.

Trevor is thinking to see if his best friend will tell him about the almost marriage proposal.

I'll give him a call later. Right now, Jasmine wants to go for a walk to the park. I think she likes a friendly dog that frequents there with his owner.

Jason is working on proposals tonight. He has a meeting in the morning with Jeremy where they are going to formalize the deal with a contract. Jason has the money to pay it all up front, but he doesn't want to put all his eggs in the basket at the same time. He will agree to parse it out over a year's time. It will also give him time to observe and see just what kind of an owner he is. The deal will be a fifty-fifty split, so he needs to be careful. They will each be equal partners once this is all done. The contract his attorney has drawn up should take care of all the extra questions Jeremy was asking about his financials. He has a right to know those that will affect the business, but he is asking things that he doesn't need to know. Jason will answer what he feels is right in the morning.

Everything has looked good so far. He has asked his attorney to add a codicil, letting him off the hook if something isn't quite right after they sign the deal. Jason is just afraid that once he signs the contract, Jeremy's true self will show through, assuming that is not him for real. Jason feels he is the one taking all the risks here.

He calls Jeremy to confirm the meeting in the morning.

"Hello, this is Jeremy."

"Jeremy, this is Jason. Just wanted to confirm we are still on for tomorrow morning. Seven a.m., right? I have the contract that my lawyer put together for this meeting. I have emailed it to you so you have a chance to read it before the meeting. Let me know if there is anything you don't agree with or if there is anything that you don't want, and I will take a look."

"Oh, I'm sure it's just fine, but I will look at it and let you know tomorrow if there is anything I am not in agreement with," Jeremy says with a great deal of enthusiasm.

Now Jeremy has his own agenda that does not include Jason. He will listen and do everything in his power tomorrow to get Jason to sign this contract. Once he does, then he can start his campaign to dismantle the company and right under Jason's nose. This process should take about two years. He will do it slowly and methodically to ensure he does not catch on. He has done it before, so he can do it again. He just needs Jason's money. If he has to do this over the course of more than a year to get all of it, then so be it. He will do what he did before—hire relatives to work in key areas of the company.

Chapter Eleven

Jimmy is deep into his investigation now. He has interviewed several key people at the museum, regarding pretty much how things work in the bowels of the museum. He wants a picture in his mind of what goes on there and how these people do their jobs. Now he will start issuing directives to other teams that will work down to the others in the building like the workers that do all the real work.

"Harvey, I need you to start with the crime scene and work your way back. Start at the dock area, and work your way into the setup room where the murder allegedly took place."

Harvey is one of the key forensic technicians that gets people to say what they didn't intend to say. That's why Jimmy wants him doing the interviews of the people that do the work and get a layout of exactly what happens down in that room besides the obvious. They send crates and packages out of the building, as well as receive the same from all over the world.

"Harvey, I want you also to go over the manifests of recent deliveries, and oh, make sure their credentials are up-to-date, and most importantly, whose credentials are they? If they are able to receive packages from overseas without it going to customs first, I want to know. And if they do, I want a really close comb-over that process. Make sure everything there is aboveboard. Any irregularities, I want a report about it. Are we clear on all that?"

Jimmy is really good at giving out orders, especially if it's something he cares about, and this he does. He cares about Trevor and does not want to see him go through more than he has to. Jimmy scratches his head, thinking Trevor is really going off the deep end on this guy he barely knows. But he has always had deep feelings right off the bat for people regardless of all the times Jimmy has warned him to go slow. He is really thinking now that he needs to check in with Trevor here in the next day or so and let him know where they are in all this so far. Jimmy has always known that Trevor was a deep-feeling person, and he has known for some time that Trevor is not exactly what most see on the surface. He just has these feelings that no one can identify with. Doesn't make him strange, just mysterious. They have been good friends for a very long time. In fact, since college days, Trevor and Jimmy have been the best of friends.

Not sure where Jason and Trevor met, but it was some time before that, Jimmy thinks.

They were inseparable in school. Jimmy and Trevor were always close. Jimmy always kind of looked out for Trevor in college. Jason and Trevor have always been like brothers.

Never got the story on where they met but they have been very close for years.

Harvey arrives at the historical museum dock area. He sees someone has locked the dock door where there should be detectives or technicians buzzing around. He bangs on the door to no answer.

Dammit, if I have to walk all the way around, I am going to be really pissed at someone.

He keeps knocking to no avail. He is going to have to walk around to the main entrance. This is at least a six- to eight-block walk if he chooses to walk. He should leave his car here since he will actually be back here after he walks around and all the way to the dock from inside.

Jeez, I knew I should have worn tennis shoes today. This is going to kill my feet. Oh well, a guy's got to do what a guy's got to do.

Harvey heads down the walk to the front door. In the meantime, there are policemen inside taking pictures of where the dead man lay and the blood all around, which was not much. Someone else was taking all the pictures of the stuff around already in the room where the man was killed, trying to paint a picture of what happened here. Since they did not have a body, they were really only speculating what and how this whole scene took place. The only person who saw the dead body was Jimmy who is a lieutenant, so they trust him. And most of them have worked for or around Jimmy for years. He's a friend, and if he saw a dead body named Christopher on the floor right there next to the workbench, then they believe him and hope he can find this body at some point during the investigation before the investigation is complete.

Well, I guess the investigation will not be complete until there is a body, Harvey thinks.

The lieutenant will be working that part of the investigation while the other teams take care of the other parts like analyzing the blood to see if there might be a match to any known suspects in their databases. There is also a team that will be working on the photos that are taken and interviewing the people who work there.

Harvey finally makes it to the front entrance of the museum and immediately finds several policemen working on one thing or another in the front and sides of the hallway to the floor downstairs. He checks in with the person coordinating and moves toward the setup and dock areas. He sees a guy walking just ahead of him wearing a uniform with some insignias on the sleeve. Assuming he is right, this must be the person who discovered the body with Jimmy.

"Hey, excuse me. Are you Rodney, the head person of this security detail that protects this museum?" Harvey hollers ahead.

The man turns around and replies, "I am Rodney, Sergeant. What can I do for you?"

"You found the body with Jimmy from our squad?"

"I did, yes, sir," Rodney responds back almost immediately. "Can I help you?"

"Well, I have a couple questions for you, if you don't mind."

"Certainly, Sergeant. Ask away."

"Could we walk and talk? I am on my way to the back west section of the museum for a look at the security desk from that door. I assume you are going to the setup area, which is halfway to where I am going."

"So what's up?"

"Well I just wanted to clarify a couple things. So when you were downstairs with Jimmy, you came into the room and you both saw the man dead on the floor half under the workbench on the far east side of the room, is that right?"

"Yeah, that's right," Rodney says.

"Okay, so when you approached the body, you told Jimmy he looked familiar, right?" Harvey says while looking at his notes.

Rodney just nods his head.

"Okay, so who actually approached the body first? You or Jimmy?"

"Jimmy saw it first and pointed it out to me."

"What about the identity of the body? According to Jimmy, you identified the body. Is that right?"

"Well, I checked for a badge and wallet from the man on the floor, and I found his museum ID badge. It told us who he was. Plus, I recognized him. I have spoken several times to him. He was always having his lunch about the time I would patrol the areas around the section he always worked at. I would stop and talk to him when I would pass his station. He was a very nice guy and sweet to everyone."

"Why didn't you recognize him right away?" Harvey asks. "Why did it take looking at his ID badge to determine you knew him?"

"Well, when we first approached him, he was facing the wall. After I saw the ID badge, I asked Jimmy if we could turn him over so I could see his face. He turned him over, and even though his face was badly bruised, I could tell it was Christopher. I was very sorry to see it was Christopher."

"So Christopher and you were friends then?"

"Well, I wouldn't say we were friends, but definitely not strangers. I would describe it as friendly, not friends."

"Okay, so let me be sure I have this straight," Harvey states. "You both walk into the room and immediately see this body on the floor. You rush to it and check to see if he was alive. You see that he is not, and you check his pockets for IDs, wallet, or some way to ID him. You find his museum ID and determine he is Christopher, whom you have had many friendly conversations with in the past.

And you recognized him as soon as you saw who he is. Is all that right so far?" Harvey exhales and waits for an answer.

"Sounds right, Sergeant."

"Okay, so what did you both do from there?" Harvey asks another follow-up question.

"Well, Jimmy is the cop. so he checked out the rest of the room to be sure we were alone."

"And were you?" Harvey asks.

"Yes, we were," Rodney answers, satisfied with how this line of questioning is going and approving the way this Harvey is handling it.

"Okay, one more question," Harvey says as they stopped near the stairs to the setup area in the lower level, "Once you determined there had been a murder down there, you and Jimmy did what?"

"Why are you not asking Jimmy these things?" Rodney asks.

"Well, I am just checking in to confirm what he told me since he is not here right now."

"Oh, okay then. Well, we left the room, closed out the lights, and after we went back upstairs, I secured the crime scene by deactivating the security doors for this section of the museum."

Harvey says, "And once the door security has been deactivated, can anyone get in a room once that has happened?"

"Absolutely not!" exclaims Rodney.

"Okay, one final question then. How do you explain the body's disappearance from that room after you two left, assuming the body was really there?" Harvey fires back.

"I can't explain that," says Rodney. "All I can tell you is that we saw the body, cleared the room, and locked it down so no one could get in after we left."

"Okay, Rodney." Harvey shakes his hand. "That's all I have for now. I may have some questions for you down the road. Will you be okay if I come back for some follow-up questions?"

"Yeah, no problem," Rodney says.

"Oh, there is one last item. Can you please send me the logs of the doors six hours before you and Jimmy found the body and the rest of the night after you locked down the rooms?" Harvey asks.

"Sure, but why six hours before?"

"Well, according to our forensic experts, the blood found on the workbench was within three to four hours old by the time my guys got here. I calculate that the blood then had to be there between four to six hours before you and Jimmy discovered the body. You see, there are a lot of things you can determine without a body. Blood is one of them. The DNA from the blood had only a short window before its properties start to change. Even though these DNA samples do not lose their potency, there are now ways we can tell approximately how long blood was splattered from someone's body. Pretty cool, huh?"

"Yeah, that's interesting," Rodney states.

"Well, I am sorry I took up so much of your time, Rodney. I think I have all I need at this point. Thanks for your help." Harvey shakes Rodney's hand again.

Harvey says one more thing before he leaves, "I appreciate your help on clearing up some questions I had. You take care, and I will catch up with you later."

One of the things that Harvey does best is ask questions he already knows the answer to so he can see if what he has is what they tell him. He does a pass-fail on them to see how they do. Everything with them is pass or fail, and Rodney failed miserably. Now he has to find out why he is so far off from the real account of what happened, which came from Jimmy. Jimmy is the best cop he knows, so he has no doubt in his mind whatsoever that Jimmy's account of what happened was completely accurate.

So why was Rodney lying about things I can easily check? Harvey thinks to himself. *There is more here than meets the eye. I need to run some facts past Jimmy when I get back. But for now, down to the crime scene to see what's going on down there.*

As Harvey approaches the bottom of the stairs, he is inundated by police officers that need his expertise.

"Hey, Harvey," says one of the technicians, "can you come over here? You have to see this. We found some hairs stuck to this wrench and a clear spot of blood with it. I think this is the tool that was used to beat him with. Some of the blood is smeared, but we can get a clear match to who this belongs to if they are in the system."

"Okay," says Harvey, "get that to the lab, and tell them I need a rush job on this. We need to see if this is in the system and can match to anyone, although I suspect that it won't because if this is Christopher's blood, I doubt that he is in the system. But you never know, do you?"

As Harvey is moving across the room, another technician approaches him with another one right behind him.

"Harvey, I took all the pictures I can for now. Everything has been photographed including where Jimmy said the body was. Do you need anything else photographed before I head back to the station?"

"If you have everything covered, then we should be good for now. I am most interested in knowing who this person was beyond his name, why he was down here so far away from where he works, and what was he mixed up in that got him killed. Plus, the million-dollar question, where is his body, and why was it moved?"

"Well, hopefully, these photos will shed some light on what went on down here and give us a time line," the technician said.

"Okay, head back to the station and let me know as soon as we have something," Harvey says. "Now what is your issue?" Harvey turns to the other technician who was waiting patiently for Harvey to finish up with the other guy.

"Well, I have been getting some samples of tire treads outside the dock door," the technician says with confidence.

"And what will that show us?" Harvey blurts out. "I mean, it's a dock. Trucks are coming and going all the time. How will tread marks outside the dock doors help us determine what happened here?"

"Well, according to the log, there have been no deliveries since the day before yesterday. But these tire tracks are fresh. Can't be more than a few hours old. If there were no deliveries, how are there fresh tread marks on the payment?"

"You know," Harvey starts out, "you could have started with there were no deliveries because now that makes sense. If there were no deliveries, how are there fresh marks? Good catch. So where did you find this log?"

"There is a log by the dock door where they log all deliveries so they know who has been here, I guess. This, according to the log, is filled out by the drivers making the delivery or, in some cases, picking up containers that are being shipped."

"Well, those pickups are the ones I would be most interested in," says Harvey. "Somehow a body was removed from here in a very short window from when Jimmy and Rodney saw the body, so we need to know how it was removed and in what type of vehicle. Do you think you can work on that piece?"

Harvey puts his hand on the technician's shoulder. This technician is really new to the department, as well as Harvey's team. He wants him to know without saying he is sorry he barked at him. He is just frustrated that there is so little to go on, and he didn't mean to take it out on the new guy.

"Jason, what's going on with you?" Trevor says into the phone. "It's been a few days. Thought I would see if you had time for some dinner and drinks tonight."

Trevor is hoping to get this whole business about Jeanette's line of work out of the way. Then he can decide if he still wants to marry her, and hopefully, it will not affect their friendship.

"I am sure I can work that into my schedule. What time were you thinking?" Jason asks.

"Let's go to our favorite haunt and say about seven p.m.," Trevor says. "Will that work? We can catch up with everything, and I can tell you how things are going with the Christopher investigation."

"Sounds good to me. I will meet you there at seven."

"Thanks, man. I was just thinking we haven't had much time to get together lately. It will be good to catch up. See you then."

As Trevor hangs up, he is wondering how he is going to bring this conversation up with Jason about Jeanette. He knows this is going to be a tough subject, and he will probably end up hating one or both of them after this.

Well, I have to tell him, Trevor thinks. *I can't let him marry her without him knowing the truth. We'll see how the conversation goes tonight. If he brings it up, maybe I will have my way into the conversation. I can't believe he wouldn't at least mention it to me. I guess I will see.*

When Jason hangs up on the phone with Trevor, he turns his attention back to Jeremy who was going through the paperwork with Jason on what's next. Jason hands Jeremy his check and asks that they both go down to the bank to deposit it so that Jeremy can have Jason added to the authorization for the account. Kill two birds, so to speak.

The phone rings while Trevor is working away at this latest decoding project for the FBI.

"Hello. This is Trevor. How can I help you?"

"Trevor Andrews?" the voice on the telephone says. "This is Greg Hubbard from the FBI minor crimes unit. Your boss, Mark Thomas, said you would be a great candidate for this. We are looking for some new blood, and from what we see on your credentials that Mark sent over, you would be a perfect match to what we are looking for. Do you think we could meet and go over some things? Qualifications, what we are looking for, how you fit, and all that—basically an interview to see if we are as much a match to you as we think you are for us."

"Mr. Hubbard, I would love to meet with you," Trevor says enthusiastically. "I can make myself available anytime you want."

"That's great, Trevor, and you can call me Greg. I was thinking end of the week. It's Monday afternoon now, say Friday around two p.m. Will that work for you?"

"That's great, Greg. Where shall I meet you?"

"That's the best part, Trevor. I will come to you. Mark said we can use one of your conference rooms. So I will be there at your office Friday at two p.m., okay?"

"Perfect, sir. I look forward to seeing you then. And, Greg, thank you so much," Trevor says with a great big smile on his face.

"You are very welcome, Trevor. I will see you then," Greg says, after which he hangs up the phone.

Trevor is just beaming with a really big grin on his face that Mark could not fail to miss. As he walks over to Trevor, Trevor shouts out that this guy Greg called and told him what the conversation was all about.

"I am so glad he called you. Although I will be sorry to see you go, this will be great for you and your career. I hope everything works out for you. Let me know if there is anything else I can do to help you with this."

Mark turns to walk away. All Trevor can think about is how amazing it will be to actually be in the spy game.

Yeah, even though they don't call it that anymore, it still fits, Trevor thinks. *Wow, how great that would be to be in this all the way. Who knows where I could go from there?*

He starts to daydream about the what-ifs.

Chapter Twelve

Jeanette starts to think Jason might not ask her again. He hasn't spoken to her since she told him, not now. She is really hoping that she didn't blow it by telling him to wait. She wonders aloud if she shouldn't call him. But what would she say to him?

I think I will just wait until he calls. She really believes he will call her before too long. She still thinks maybe she should call Trevor to see what he thinks, and then at the same time, she can maybe see what he has done about telling Jason.

As he is walking out his door to meet Jason, Trevor hears the phone ring and decides to run and get it in case it is Jason.

"Hello," Trevor says picking up the phone.

"Trevor, hi, this is Jeanette. I wondered if I could run something by you really quick."

"Sure, Jeanette. What's on your mind?"

"Well, I haven't spoken to Jason since I told him to wait before asking me what I know he was going to ask me. Truth is, I am worried. He hasn't called or even tried to get ahold of me since. I was kind of hoping you had some words of encouragement for me. Tell me I am being ridiculous or something."

"What I can tell you is that I am having dinner and drinks with him shortly. In fact, I was on my way there when you called. I will do what I can but no promises. I am just going to see if the subject comes up, which I am certain it will, but I am also going to see if this is the right time to tell him. I will play it by ear. If it looks like he is in the mood, then I will. Like I said, no promises."

"I understand. I really do. I am just afraid he just won't ask me again."

"Do you really think that's all it will take to make him back off? Really?" Trevor says with as much kindness as he could muster. "I have to go. You know, to meet Jason! I will let you know if anything happens, okay?" Trevor tries to hang up.

"Got it. I will back off so you can talk to him, and hopefully, he will call me soon. Thanks, Trevor. I will wait to hear from you. Talk to you later. Enjoy your dinner."

"Thanks, Jeanette. Good night. I will talk to you tomorrow."

"Jason, over here. How are you, man?" Trevor says as Jason walks over to him. "Been a while. How are things going with Jeremy? Are they moving along? Have you invested yet? Sorry, Jason. Don't know what I was thinking. We got plenty of time to talk about everything you got going. Here, let's get you a drink."

"Thanks, Trevor. I know you want to know everything that's going on with me, but yeah, can you just give me a minute?" Jason says as the waiter brings him a beer.

"Are you gentlemen ready to order?" the waiter asks.

"Yeah, I think I am," Trevor says and gives the waiter his order, as does Jason.

They hand the menus back to the waiter and proceed to sip on their beer.

"So, Trevor, I can't prove it, but I think this Jeremy is a crook," Jason says, kind of quiet.

"Really? What makes you think that?"

"Well, get this. I have already given him my first installment of the investment, right? Well, three weeks later, I was looking over the books for something that one of the guards asked me about, and I noticed the investment money I put up was nowhere on the financial reports, nowhere."

"Could it be on some other financial ledger maybe? Not trying to make excuses for him but you don't know everything that's going on in this business yet. Don't you think you should give him the benefit of the doubt and ask him about it? Just see what he says about it."

"No, you are right. I just get nervous when I am putting up so much of my own money here," Jason responds. "But get this, the bookkeeper is his sister, and the captain is his cousin who makes all the decisions regarding who goes where and what we spend on what. It just seems not exactly aboveboard, and I can't put my finger on it. Trevor, I just have this awful feeling in my gut that something is off here."

"Have you spoken to him about this? Maybe there's a perfectly logical explanation." Trevor tries calming him down, but Jason is getting excitable. "Look, I am not making excuses for this guy. I am just saying let's not jump to conclusions without knowing all the facts. And you do not know all the facts. When is that next investment payment due?"

"In three months," Jason answers.

"Well, why don't you do this? Before you give him any more money, sit down and talk to him. Make sure all your questions and suspicions are satisfied before you pay him another dime," Trevor says rather finally with a fist to the table.

"Okay, you're right, you're right. I am getting upset for nothing. Sorry about that, old friend. So how did you get so smart?"

"I'm going to forget you said that, buddy," says Trevor with a grin. "So tell me how things are going with you and Jeanette. Not to change the subject abruptly but you aren't going to get any answers from the Jeremy situation tonight, so let's talk about something else, like Jeanette."

"We're doing all right, I guess," Jason says, kind of quiet and under his breath.

"Okay, what's wrong, Jason? Dude, I know you remember? When you talk into your hand like that, you have something on your mind. So what's going on? You two having issues?"

"Damn you, you know me too well. Okay, so I sort of asked her to marry me."

"You what? Are you out of your mind? What do you mean you asked her to marry you?"

"Okay, okay, well, I didn't actually ask her, but I was about to, and Jeanette stopped me. Told me she knew what I was going to ask her and told me to stop. She said she wants to marry me more than anything but not right now. But she made me promise to ask her again."

"Jason, I had no idea you were getting this serious. What do you know about her anyway? I mean, it seems to me you are jumping into this rather quickly without knowing much about each other. I mean, really, Jason, what do you know about her? Where does she work? Who are her friends? Have you met anyone she works with or any of her friends? Don't you think you are rushing this a bit? Don't you think you should—oh, I don't know—know a little more about her? Just a thought, dude. Marriage is a big deal. I just don't want you making a rash decision that turns into a mistake down the road. Okay, I said my piece. I will stop badgering you now. What else is going on with you?" Trevor says to Jason, hoping to change the subject again.

They sit there in relative silence while they eat their dinner and drink their drinks. It gets a little uncomfortable for them right now, so a little small talk will hopefully pave the way a little. Trevor is thinking that this is probably not the right time to bring up about Jeanette's livelihood. He thinks he has pissed him off now. Challenging his feelings for Jeanette might not have been the right way to go on this.

It's been too quiet, so Jason decided to break the ice a bit and really get the subject changed back to Trevor. "So, Trevor, how goes the investigation into Christopher's murder? Any word from Jimmy on where they are at with all that?"

"I actually haven't talked to Jimmy for a couple days now," says Trevor. "Not sure where he's at with it, but I was thinking if I don't hear from him by, say, tomorrow, I will call him. He did tell me that he can't keep me involved like we had agreed. He's afraid it's going to get a little too dangerous, and his captain does not want civilians poking around where they don't belong. I mean, I get that. I just want to know what they are doing and if there is anything I can help them with. That's all."

"Well, I'm sure when he has something to tell you, he will call and give you an update," Jason replies.

"You're right. Let's go. I got to get up early tomorrow. My boss put me in this new position last week. I am really excited about it. It's actually doing investigations with some of the agencies we do business with. It's a great opportunity. I have my first interview tomorrow, so I want to be fresh for it."

"You'll be great. That is great news. Good luck. Call me to let me know how it goes," Jason says as they are walking out the door. Jason walks Trevor to his car talking about what this could mean for Trevor.

"Speak of the devil," Trevor says under his breath.

Jimmy is waiting for Trevor in his driveway.

"Hey, Trevor!" Jimmy yells across the lawn.

"Jimmy, I was just talking about you to Jason. We were wondering where you are in this investigation about Christopher."

"Let's go inside. I do have some stuff to tell you, and you might be able to help me."

Jimmy says as they walk into his house, "Okay, so, Trevor, I have a couple of things you might be able to help me with."

"Yeah, no problem. What can I do?"

"Well, first, you can tell me a little about Christopher. What does he do at the museum? Why do you think he was down in the dock area, an area he clearly does not work in?"

"Truth be told, Jimmy, I really don't know that much about what Christopher does, much less why he would be down in the docks. I know he set up displays that were brought up from the setup area. He did tell me that much. Maybe there was something wrong with a display or something, and he had to go down and clear it up. I mean, I really have no idea."

"You told me that he was suspicious of something that was going on down in that area a few weeks ago," Jimmy remarks. "Could he have gone down to investigate it and got caught and killed for his trouble?"

"I guess anything is possible," Trevor says. "I can tell you from my impressions of that conversation that I think he was too scared to check things out as you say."

"It's more likely that someone saw him snooping and grabbed him," Jimmy says. "And that got him killed for his trouble. Well, a couple of things have come to light. There is a log at the dock that the drivers fill out so they can account for their time at the dock, and there were no trucks for deliveries in or out of the museum in the past two days, again according to the logs, but there were fresh tire tracks outside the dock doors. Someone was there, and it wasn't logged, so that tells me it wasn't aboveboard or a legitimate stop." Jimmy says all this with a troubled look on his face.

"Okay, so that tells us someone was there," Trevor says. "I don't know what else I can tell you. I really didn't know Christopher that well. What we had in common were our dogs. I stopped by there one night after we met. He was going to give me a quick tour, but we never got around to that."

"Okay, well, that's about all I have for right now," Jimmy says as he gets up to leave. "That pretty much brings you up-to-date on where we are at. I have to get going. Got to check in with my key people to see where we are at and figure out what our next move is going to be."

Jimmy shakes Trevor's hand and says, "I will keep you posted as best as I can. Talk to you later."

As Trevor is getting ready for bed, he lets Jasmine back in the house from the backyard when, just then, the phone rings. Trevor thinks to himself, *Any bets on who this is?*

"Hello."

"Trevor, this is Jeanette. I thought I would call and check in to see how dinner went with Jason," Jeanette says rapidly, trying not to seem to anxious or pushy.

"Well, I wasn't able to tell him. It just didn't seem to be the right time. He does plan to call you and soon, so there is that," Trevor tries to tell her as gently as he can without telling her much at all. "I will find another time to tell him about your little secret."

"Good morning, Jimmy," Harvey says as Jimmy walks through the door. "When you have a few minutes, I would like to talk to you about the investigation into the museum murder."

"Give me five seconds so I can get my coffee, and we can chat," Jimmy says as he pours himself a hot cup of coffee. "So what have you learned so far?" Jimmy asks Harvey as he sips his coffee.

"Jimmy, how well do you know this Rodney that runs the security force at the museum?"

"Not that well, I'm afraid. I used to know him really well, but we lost touch for some time. I hadn't spoken to him in years until this investigation came up. I started this off as a favor for a friend. I was asked to look into what was going on at the museum by an old friend. It started out as just an inquiry into some trouble that his friend Christopher had possibly gotten himself into. Had no idea it would turn into his murder. I decided I can check into this discretely because I knew Rodney."

"So you really haven't spoken to him in a very long time, so you don't know him anymore," Harvey says.

"Yeah, that's pretty much it. Why do you ask?"

"Well, there is something off about this guy. Can't put my finger on it exactly, but he is lying about something. I just need to figure out what I think is off and move on. I do need to know if you are all right with me doing what I need to in order to get this solved."

"Yeah, I'm all right with that. I have no loyalty to this guy. If you think there is something off about Rodney, do what you have to. I really want to solve this for my friend, Trevor. He really liked this guy Christopher and was hoping to get to know him better. Now he won't, so if we can find out what happened and get him some answers, I know he would feel somewhat better. Not great but better."

"Great. Thanks, Jimmy. I will keep you posted on what I learn."

"Jeremy, where do we stand with this setup?" Jason says as he walks into the office. "I still don't see any evidence in our accounts that I invested a dime. Now why is that?"

Jeremy ponders on this for a moment and says, "There is a perfectly logical explanation for that. Your investment money went to pay outstanding bills that needed to get paid in order to do things like keep the lights on."

"There was nothing about that in anything I read before I invested," Jason says, raising his voice. "I was investing in this business so I can be a part of it, not to pay your bills. What kind of crap is this?"

Jeremy starts to walk away, but Jason follows him to his office, which is toward the back of the building. "I want an answer for this, Jeremy. Explain this to me."

"Jason, I am very sorry that I wasn't completely honest with you about the need for investment money to cover my bills. Please don't let this sway you from your investment in this business. It really is a great business and a good opportunity for you. Will it help if I promise in the future to be completely honest with everything we do?"

"Had you explained it to me, I would have been all right with it. What I am pissed about is that you attempted to deceive me—that, I don't like. I will accept your explanation as long as it doesn't happen again. I want complete honesty moving forward. Agreed?" Jason states quite firmly.

"Yes, sir, I can agree with that," Jeremy states as they shake hands.

"Okay, so from now on, we are involved together in any financial decisions this company needs to make?" Jason asks.

"Okay, so we can move on from here. There are decisions regarding the operations that we need to talk about," Jeremy says as he moves to his office chair. "Now that we got that settled, let's talk about this operation and how we can improve it. I have some ideas."

Chapter Thirteen

"Trevor," Mark Thomas says as he approaches Trevor's desk. "This is Greg Hubbard. I believe you were expecting him."

Trevor rises and shakes Greg's hand vigorously, grinning from ear to ear. "Greg, it's great to meet you in person. I am really excited for this opportunity. Thank you so much. Also, thanks so much to you, Mark. I know this would never have happened if it weren't for you, so I can't thank you enough. This is a dream come true."

"Trevor," Mark says, "you haven't got it yet. You need to sit down and talk to Greg, but he is encouraged by what I have already told him, so don't disappoint."

"I won't, Mark. Sorry, I just get really excited when there is something I want, and it's right there in front of me. Greg, I think we can talk in here."

Trevor directs Greg to a conference room.

"Thanks, Trevor, and I understand your excitement. I remember when I was first considered for this position I am looking at you for, I was excited also, so don't ever be afraid to show me how excited you are for this. Let's talk about what I am looking for and if you are as much of a fit as I think you are." Greg starts to explain what he is actually looking for and how Trevor fits into those plans. "Let's start off with how you see this position for you and what you feel you can bring to the table now that you know what it is we are looking for."

"Harvey," Jimmy calls from across the room, "I am doing an FBI search of this guy Rodney. I want to see, first and foremost, if this guy has a past and if there are any skeletons in his closet. The FBI is currently doing a background search for anything that pops up from what he has done in the past, although I am not expecting to find anything because I checked with the historical museum main office and found that they do background checks annually for all their employees and FBI background checks for their security personnel. It took a lot of research to find even that.

"Since the historical museum is one of the largest museums with all their branches, research offices, libraries, and leadership teams for everything, it took a bit to find what and who I was looking for, but I finally found the right department. It seems Rodney has been with the museum for many years and has had a spotless record since day 1. He made his way to the management level, running the security force about three years ago when the previous manager was fired for misappropriating funds or something like that.

"They were not real forthcoming about the incident, but they were able to tell me that much. So he is above reproach according to the leadership at the museum. And those were their words, not mine. So where does that get us?" Jimmy asks.

Jimmy is thinking that this does not surprise him. He has always thought that Rodney has been very good at what he does.

"The one thing I can't wrap my head around, though, is that according to Rodney, once the security doors are locked out for a specific area, no one can get in," Harvey says. "So, Jimmy, how do you think someone was able to remove a body and almost all evidence it was there without the security panels catching them?"

"Truth is, I have no idea. What I think is that the security doors are not as impregnable as Rodney says they are. They can't be. Someone removed a body from that room and left practically no evidence. That tells me someone was in that room right after we left.

"You know what, Harvey, I just got a thought. Ask Rodney if the security doors will log if someone leaves the room after they were in there. What if there was someone in that setup area while we were down there? And after we left, they removed the body and all evidence. See if that's possible. If it is, then your next stop is to find out where they would have been able to hide while I was doing a room search. I know how to do a room search, so I would not have missed anything obvious. But I don't know this place, so is it possible that there are places to hide that are completely oblivious to anyone unfamiliar.

"These are questions you can get answers to without Rodney. Go check out the room yourself. You should be able to get back in there without Rodney because our forensic people are still there. But you need to hurry. They are almost done in there and will be leaving. Give Gabe a call and tell him you are on your way and to delay his departure. He is the head of our forensic team working in the dock area. He can drag it out a bit until you get there—that is, if they are ready to leave but I think they are. So call him now and head back over there."

Gabe is a big guy that is as gentle as a lamb according to several of the peers he works with. Gabe is in his sixties and is ready to retire as he says all the time. He has been working in forensics for forty years and has seen it all. He is ready to sit on a beach sipping cool adult beverage and living the rest of his life without worrying about what a crime scene has for evidence that he can collect. He is tired of getting up and going work.

Time to retire, he thinks. And he keeps thinking that every time he goes to a new crime scene.

He is working in the dock area right now and has collected some great samples of hair and dirt from the floor as his cell phone rings.

"Gabe, this is Harvey. I need to come back out there and check a couple of things. Are you almost done out there?"

"Yeah, in fact, the team is wrapping things up and getting their gear together so we can get out of here. So what's up?" Gabe cradles his phone as he is putting things in his many cases.

"Well, do me a favor, will you? Delay your departure. Find a reason to stay until I get there. I need to get back in there without security upstairs knowing about it. Can you do that for me, Gabe?" Harvey says, running to his car.

"Sure, no sweat. Come back to the dock, and I will let you in. Just knock on the dock door. Security will see you on their monitors, but they will think you are just part of our team, completing things with us. How soon can you be here?"

"It will take me about twenty minutes to get there. Thanks, Gabe. I appreciate your help on this. You might also be able to help me once I get in there. I will fill you in once I get there, and we will see if I am right about a couple of things. See you soon."

"Jeanette. Hello, darling. It's Jason. I know I should have called sooner, but I was a little put off. Nothing against you but I was a little pissed that you stopped me from proposing to you, which I spent a great deal of time preparing for. I guess my feelings were a little hurt. But I am over that now after talking it out with Trevor. So how about dinner tonight?"

"No, I don't think so. Too bad. You blew it." Jeanette laughs. "Just kidding. I am so glad you called. I was so worried that you wouldn't call me again. I am really glad you did. I would love to go out to dinner with you tonight. Where were you thinking?" Jeannette answers with as much enthusiasm as she could muster, exhaling with a big sigh of relief that he called her, thanks to whatever Trevor said to him.

"I will pick you up in an hour or so. Six p.m.? Can you be ready, or should we make it later?"

"I can be ready. I am always ready for you, handsome!"

As Jason gets ready for his date, the restaurant calls that he made reservations at to tell him there might be a little wait when they get there. They just seated a big party. Nothing to worry about though. They just wanted him to know.

Jason has prepared a great night for Jeanette: First, dinner at one of the hottest places in town. All the politicians go there. A place called Rasika's. It's supposed to be a real hot spot for the city's politicians, specifically Democrats. Not that he cares about all that and he's sure that Jeanette could not care less but they are supposed to have great food and a very romantic ambience or at least a quieter atmosphere.

We will see, Jason thinks. *They were very accommodating. So hopefully there won't be too much of a wait.*

This is probably why they wanted his phone number when he made the reservation. He will go pick her up shortly.

"So, Trevor, I have really enjoyed this interview," Greg says, wrapping up the interview he just had with Trevor. "We seem to be the right place for you. I would like to officially offer you a position with our agency as a junior special agent. Just so you know, you are only a junior agent until you complete your training. Your training will be at the FBI headquarters at Quantico, Virginia. For right now, just keep doing what you are doing, and I will be in touch. For the record, I have offered you a position as an agent with the FBI. I need you to accept or decline the position for the record."

"I, for the record, officially accept your offer for a position with the FBI as a junior agent," Trevor says very formally with a huge smile on his face.

"I will reach out to Mark tomorrow and let him know what we are doing. But I would assume he is expecting to lose you sometime in the very near future. Since it's late, I believe he has probably gone home. I am sorry I kept you so long, but this was a great interview and I think you will be a great addition to our team."

"Thank you so much, Greg," Trevor says as he shakes his hand while they walk toward the front door. "I will wait to hear from you."

Greg walks out the door. With Trevor being on the verge of the career of his dreams, he almost feels guilty because of what happened to Christopher.

Harvey runs toward the dock door where Gabe is standing, holding the door open for him.

"Hey, Gabe, thanks for waiting for me." Harvey walks through the door and says, "Thanks."

"So what are you looking for, Harvey?" Gabe asks, walking behind him as he walks in past the dock area to the setup area.

This is where Gabe and his crew have mostly been working, sifting through blood splatters and hair fragments and such.

"Well, Jimmy thinks that there might have been someone hiding in this area somewhere when he searched it before. He cleared the room, but he thinks that there is a hiding place somewhere down here that someone unaware of what goes on down here would not see or find right off. So what I want to do is look further. And I could use your help. What I want to do is look at every inch of this place. You and me only. I don't want a bunch of people running about. You and me searching every inch. You up for that?"

Harvey and Gabe walk toward the setup area where the body was found.

"Jimmy believes there has to be someplace down here we can't see," Harvey says with this weird look on his face like he doesn't really believe it. But Jimmy is his superior. He does what he is told. "There is an explanation why someone was able to move a body after they left here. We just have to find it."

Gabe starts opening cabinet doors and going through everything as Harvey takes the other side of the room.

Rodney is watching on the cameras in the control room and seems nervous. He has a pretty good idea what this Harvey is doing. He is pretty sure he was careful enough to hide everything he was doing from everyone that has been down there. After all, no one knows this place better than him. Getting rid of that body didn't have the results he was hoping for.

I guess Jimmy is more respected than I thought, Rodney thinks, *and as such, when he says he saw a body, they believe him and will pursue an investigation without a body for now. At some point though, they are going to have to come up with a body. This investigation will go nowhere. How could it continue to long when there is nothing really for them to go on? They are certainly buying my lies about the security system. Since I am in charge, no one even thought to ask anyone else the questions I was asked by this Harvey. He is a really thorough cop though. There were a couple of times I thought they were going to uncover something I didn't want them to find. Well, this latest little escapade with Harvey and this other guy will have to run its course. They can look all they want but they won't find a damn thing. I have seen to that. With my spotless record, no one is going to question me or what I have done or am doing. There is way too much at stake for me to start making mistakes now. Getting rid of the body the way I did was brilliant. No one is going to figure that out. Never. I would be so surprised if anyone even finds the body in this lifetime.*

He chuckles to himself.

This is the perfect place for the drug trade in this town. No one would ever suspect that drugs would be going through here like a supermarket. After all this is the historical museum, one of the larger museums. Security here is so tight that nothing comes through here without security knowing. And my career is above reproach. How cool is that. Rodney watches Harvey and Gabe check out a room they will find nothing in.

"Gabe, are you seeing anything?" Harvey says from across the room.

"No, I have opened up a couple of crates that were not completely sealed, but there's nothing but old relics in them," Gabe says from back across the room too. "Nothing suspicious. I am checking out these cabinets that are over next to this workbench in this other room over here. Looks like it's out of the path of everything we were doing down here all day, so I thought I would have a peek. Are you seeing anything? What about those doors over there?" Gabe points to the far wall to Harvey's right.

"I was just moving in to look at them. They look like closets to me, but I can't believe Jimmy would not have looked in the obvious places like closets, cabinets, and other places like these. Never hurts to look again, does it?"

"Nope," says Gabe.

Harvey and Gabe really didn't find anything in this room or any adjoining rooms that have closets or cabinets. They searched everything that was big enough to hide a person of average height. Nothing. This was a total bust.

"Well, Gabe, sorry I kept you. I found nothing. Not even a hint that anyone was here or had been in here. You find anything?"

"Naw, it was just as empty as what you found. I didn't even find that they have been building displays or anything new. Isn't that what this area is used for?" Gabe asks quizzically. "I mean if this happened a few days ago, doesn't business go on as normal? I have seen no evidence that anything has been done down here for days."

"So no new setups or anything?" Harvey says.

"I wonder who we can ask about that," Gabe responds back.

"That would be a question for Jimmy to pursue. I will let him know what we found and see if he can find out who would be the person in charge of building set displays and whether they have had none to build in the past week or why there is no evidence of activity in that area. Either way, Gabe, thanks for your help. I think we can call it a day for now. I also think we can release this room back to the museum. Let's get out of here."

They leave by way of the dock door. Gabe makes sure it's secure when they close it. He promised security he would make sure it was closed and secure when he left.

As Jason gets to Jeanette's door, he rings the bell to her opening it up almost immediately as though she were waiting for him by the door. She gives him a huge hug and kisses him like she has not seen him for days. It's been two days, that's all.

"Hi, honey," she says to Jason. "I am so happy to see you. Did you want to just go, or did you want to come in for a bit? I am ready to go if you are."

"Wow, I need to go away for a couple of days more often if I'm going to get this kind of reception. I missed you too. I am actually a little hungry, so if you are ready, we can go now. I was looking at the reviews for this restaurant, and it has gotten some pretty good reviews. It is more of a political hot spot though, according to what I read. I don't know about all that, but I hear the food is really good there and the ambience is supposed to be pretty special as well. So I guess we will see."

They ride to the restaurant in pretty much silence until they get there.

"We may have to wait a few minutes for our table," Jason says to try to break the silence. "They called me a while ago to let me know there might be a wait even though we have a reservation. They had to seat a huge party. But they will do the best they can and will get us seated as quickly as they can."

"Not a problem," Jeanette says. "I think we can probably wait a few. Will give us a chance to talk."

Chapter Fourteen

Twenty weeks later…

"Welcome home, Trevor!" Jason says to as he hugs his friend and shakes his hand.

Jason missed his friend. Trevor has been gone for a long time, training at the Quantico FBI training headquarters. A lot has happened while he was gone.

"Tonight Jeanette and I are taking you out to dinner and drinks to celebrate your returning home and in one piece. In the meantime, enjoy your homecoming," Jason says as he is walking out the door. "I know it's early and you want to get settled in. We will be by to pick you up in about an hour or so."

"Sounds good, Jason. Thanks. Oh, and thanks for picking me up at the airport. I was fine with taking a cab, but I did appreciate this more. I will see you in about an hour. You know I can meet you at the restaurant. You don't have to pick me up," Trevor says actually hoping he doesn't decide that's better. He would rather have Jason pick him up.

The last few months have been grueling, and he was happy to just relax for a while. He was told that he will receive a call from his new boss, Greg, shortly, letting him know what's next for him. For now, he will just relax and enjoy being home. Trevor thinks he missed Jasmine more than anyone.

Jason sure took great care of her while he was gone, Trevor thinks. *She looks great.*

"Jeanette, let's go. I told Trevor we would pick him up thirty minutes ago."

"Okay, okay, I'm coming," Jeanette says as she rushes toward the door.

As she climbs into the passenger side of the car, she asks, "So are you going to tell Trevor that we are engaged?"

"I was thinking that wouldn't be the lead story but, for sure, part of the conversation tonight. I really want to hear how his training went. He is now a full-fledged FBI agent, something he has wanted for as long as I have known him. And that has been a very long time."

"Well, I am very happy for him. Do you think this will take his mind off his friend Christopher?"

"Maybe for the past few months probably. But now he got back from his training, I am sure he will want to check in with Jimmy to see where they are at and if they have found out who killed his friend yet."

Jason is actually hoping Trevor doesn't bring it up tonight, but he is certain he will. He has checked in a couple of times with Jimmy while he was gone, and they haven't made a great deal of headway.

As they approached Trevor's house, Jason says to Jeanette, "So do you want to go get him? I can wait here."

"Sure," she says.

As she approaches the door, she rings the bell to an anxious, hungry FBI agent. After giving Trevor a big hug and kiss, she says, "So how is the handsomest FBI agent around doing tonight?"

"He's doing pretty good. He wants to get to work and actually start being an FBI agent," Trevor says rather matter-of-factly. "So how are you doing these days? It appears that he has called you and you are off to where you were before. I told you he would call you."

"I know, I know. You are always right, and I have missed you. I know Jason did. Listen, he won't tell you this, so you have to pry it out of him, but quickly Jeremy is really taking Jason for a ride and keeps making excuses for why so much money is missing from the company—missing money that can't be explained. But I did not tell you this. I just felt you needed to know. You are a federal agent now, so worm it out of him at some point, but I am worried. Please, Trevor. Jason trusts you."

"Don't worry, Jeanette. I will talk to him, and he will never know you said anything to me."

"Thanks, Trevor. He trusts you, and if you tell him what he needs to do, especially given your new occupation, he will listen to you."

"Don't worry. You got it. So let's go have a great dinner and some drinks as friends."

"Jimmy, unless Rodney has an explanation, he is lying," Harvey says as he walks in the door of the precinct with Jimmy. "I told you that three months ago, and every time I talk to that guy, I feel he is not telling me the truth or at least not everything."

"And I told you that he wasn't that good of a friend, so do what you have to."

"Okay, but he keeps playing that 'I'm friends with Jimmy' card. Practically stops me in my tracks because I think I am treading on some sacred friendship or something."

"Well, you are not, so do what you need to do. I don't care at this point. I would like to get this case moving again. It seems it's stalled. Plus, I need to go give Trevor a progress report now that he's back from Quantico. Now he is a full-time FBI field agent."

God, I am so proud of that guy, Jimmy thinks. What *an accomplishment. You want something so bad? You just go out and get it. Awesome. What a career move. Well, I will have to give him a couple days at least. I am sure he is making the rounds, and I am certain if I don't get to him, he will get to me at some point.*

"Harvey, what is the current lie or lie of omission from Rodney at this point in the investigation?" Jimmy asks.

"Well he is currently stating that there was no body in the setup area at all and that you made it all up."

"Really, I made it all up? Okay then. So where do we go from here? Since I am a big fat liar, then what did I see in the setup area? Please? Did he really think you were that stupid you would buy that line of shit?" Jimmy throws his arms up in the air.

"Well, Jimmy, I believe you, and so does everyone around here that knows you."

"I thank you all for that. So what is your next move?" Jimmy asks Harvey, who is now surrounded by several of his fellow law enforcement officers.

"Well, there are still several reasons why Rodney is good for this. One, his knuckles and hands were almost as beat up as Christopher's face. He explains this away as during his job he had to crank several handles that are in close proximity to walls and other close quarter equipment and that he had two people work for him vouch for that. And he showed them to me. I am allowing that for the moment, but I am telling you, there is something here that doesn't quite jibe. Honestly, I can't put my finger on it completely, but there is something here. He is not being as cooperative as he wants us to think he is being.

"Another thing, I found out that when the doors are locked down, they are not locked down to everyone. There are those that do actually have access—what they call emergency access—and I am certain Rodney is one of those. Why wouldn't he be? He is the commander of that security force. I would only assume that he would have complete control and access. When I learned there was a possibility, I knew it. I just can't prove it, but I will. I have requested a complete copy of all access for this entire building and all surrounding buildings from their express office in the Capital room 2300 in Washington, DC. I should have that in a couple days." Harvey shakes his finger. "I know he is hiding something. I just know he is."

"Well, what are your plans in the meantime?" Jimmy asks.

"Here's what we know at this point. We figured out how the body left the setup area: In a crate. It was shipped. We just don't know where and when. We have a time line that is pretty accurate. You and Rodney left there at six p.m. We arrived there at about six forty-five p.m. So there is about a forty-five-minute time frame there where the body and the setup room were left completely alone, so we assume. The truth is, he wasn't alone.

"Suppose, for the sake of argument, Rodney has a way to get into this room after the doors are secured, for emergencies of course.

Rodney goes down to that door at the stairwell, and with or without help, he moved the body into a crate that was leaving shortly for parts unknown, and it was sealed as if it were going out. Now I also found out that once an overseas shipment is ready for customs stamps, it's moved to another part of the dock area, in a pickup zone for the customs drivers to come in on a route and scoop up the crates that are ready.

"Now this is the historical museum. Wouldn't it make a certain amount of sense that everything they send off domestic or overseas would be above reproach? Do you think if it were to come from there, they would open up the boxes? So let's say they open a couple of the crates just to make certain. Would they open all of them or maybe just the top two or bottom two? After all, they are loading these into a truck. They are probably going to a ship that is taking them overseas or an airport. We can easily find out if there was any freight going to the airport or the shipyard that day."

"I don't see how it would be conclusive though," Jimmy pipes up.

"You're right, but at least we would know that some shipments did go out of there that day and we would be closer than we are right now. Plus, even if they didn't have a crate listed on the manifests at the museum because of what was in it, customs certainly wouldn't let it go out of there without it being on a manifest somewhere like on the ship or airplane, whichever way it went. So think about this. There is proof somewhere that there is an extra crate somewhere. I'm telling you, that is how they got a body out of there so fast. It's the only way I can see. You're a detective, what do you think?" Harvey pretty much cornered Jimmy into an answer.

Harvey gets really excited when he thinks he's onto something and when he is sure he is right. And he sounds sure he's right too. Jimmy couldn't argue most of the points he made. He was on to something here. Now the only thing is, he has to prove it. He will figure out what the hell is going on in that place one way or another, and he is sure Rodney is in the middle of whatever it is.

"Tell you what, Harvey, you bring me all the proof I need, and if I agree and I can't refute it *and* if I can make it stick, then and only then will I arrest Rodney. But we are a long way from that right now. You have a lot of legwork to do before you even get close to me making an arrest of anyone, much less Rodney. Your logic seems sound, but can you prove it and prove it all the way? That's what you need to do before I will approach Rodney with anything. He is not my best friend, but he is a friend, and even if he weren't, I would treat him to the same rights any one of us would have. Is he guilty? Maybe, but I don't know that, and neither do you. Get me proof, and then we will see. In the meantime, I am going to call it a night. I should have been home an hour ago. I will see all of you in the morning."

"Don't worry, Harvey," says the skinny detective who was hanging on his every word when he was talking to Jimmy. He didn't dare interrupt, but he was definitely interested. "If you bring him his proof, he will have to act on it. That's his job. So just get him what he needs, and you should be home free." The skinny detective called out over his shoulder, "Good night, Harvey."

"So, Trevor, tell us all about your training. Was it hard? You obviously made it. So it must have been bearable."

"It was horrible. The training was incredible. They train you on everything from the fundamentals of law to counterterrorism to counterintelligence to weapons of mass destruction. We learn about cyber and criminal investigations, including a lot of classroom training like interviewing suspects and behavioral science and stuff like that. A lot of heavy stuff like that. I'm just glad I survived. Let's just say that I am prepared to do whatever I need to do in order to be a great FBI agent. I am so stoked, Jason. I can't even begin to tell you how excited I am to be in this spot right now.

"I get my first assignment tomorrow. The guy that interviewed me is going to be my out-of-Quantico trainer. It turns out we have a trainer for a short time after we get out of training to acclimate us to the real world. So Greg will be with me for a while. I will be working with the Drug Enforcement Administration as a partner in an ongoing investigation. He will fill me in in the morning. I guess there will be some DEA officers at the field office for us to go over the case with. There will be seven of us from the FBI, and there are already five from the DEA. I guess this is a huge case. Huge amounts of dope going in and out of DC. Well, not going to worry about it tonight. Going to enjoy your company and the chance to relax finally after the grueling twenty weeks of intense training. They keep you moving the whole time. You get very little time to yourself. So this is nice.

"So fill me in on what's been going on here while I have been gone. You two seem rather tight, at least tighter than you were when I left. Things going well?"

Trevor already knows the answer.

Jeanette jumps up and says, "Jason asked me to marry him, and I said yes."

"That's awesome, guys. Congrats." Trevor shakes Jason's hand and half hugs Jeanette. "So have you set a date yet?" Trevor hopes it's far into the future.

"Actually, it's in four months."

"That seems a bit fast doesn't it?" Trevor says kind of harshly. He didn't mean for it to be so harsh, but they aren't giving Trevor any time to tell Jason what he needs to tell him about Jeanette before he marries her.

"Well, I am very happy for you both. I am sure you will be happy," he says. "Well, I hate to be a party pooper, but my career starts in the morning, and I want to be fresh for it, so I was thinking I want to get in early and get a good night's sleep. You guys can stay here, but I have to go. See you tomorrow or sometime in the next day or so."

"Oh, Trevor! We drove you."

Trevor smiles and looks back at them. "Oh yeah. I ain't going anywhere without you, am I? Okay, can we go then?"

"Sure, just messing with you. Let's go," Jason says as he gets up and escorts Jeanette from the table like a perfect gentleman.

They walk out of the restaurant in complete silence. They get into Jason's car the same way, in silence, almost like they ran out of things to say to each other. They spoke some idle chitchat in the car on the ride home, and when they got to Trevor's house, he said his goodbyes and headed toward the door.

Jason backed the car out of the driveway and into the street. "Jeanette, do you think I can spend the night at your house? I was just thinking it has been a while, and I don't have to get up early tomorrow unless you do."

"Nope. I don't have to get up at all tomorrow if I didn't want to. So yes, you can spend the night."

Jason had this idea of a very sexual and passionate evening tonight, and he plans on making sure that it ends up his way. He really wants Jeanette tonight. It has been way too long. Oh, they have had sex, but nothing passionate or what he considers really together as a couple. Since they are getting married, he feels that there should be more passion at this time in their relationship. So he wants to get that spark back no matter what.

"Jeanette, my dear love, I have wanted you since I woke up this morning. I love Trevor, but I couldn't wait until we dropped him off so I can have you to myself." Jason holds her tight by the butt cheeks.

"Jason, I wanted to tear your clothes off in the restaurant," Jeanette says while she is frantically kissing Jason all over his face and neck.

"Oh, baby, let's go into the bedroom. I want to tear off your clothes and ravage you," Jason says, now quite out of breath.

He leads Jeanette to the bedroom as he is helping her off with her clothes. As he makes his way into the bedroom, her blouse is on the carpet in the hallway and her shoes are in different spots in the house. One shoe is by the front door, and the other is in front of the couch. Jason's shirt is lying next to Jeanette's blouse in the hallway.

As he enters the bedroom, he hops as he gets his legs out of his pants, and as he does, his pants end up in front of the bed. Jeanette is now completely naked, and Jason throws her on the bed and then jumps on top of her and starts kissing her from her lips to the neck and then down her body until he gets to the best part of the buffet, as he calls it, her pubic bush and what it reveals beneath. He starts kissing her vagina like it really is part of a buffet, like it's the main course. In the meantime, he is as hard as he has probably been in the past month. He was ready to penetrate her and penetrate and penetrate.

He was ready to ravage, and she was so ready she was spreading her legs for him to easily enter. This whole process from start to where they are right now took less than five minutes, maybe six.

As they lay next to each other wrapped in each other's arms, completely spent, Jason says, "When did you want to get married? We really haven't discussed in detail when we wanted to actually get married. You know, set a date that we can tell people. We have said approximate time frames but no actual date. This is something the bride is supposed to have on their minds all the time once they get engaged. I know we are engaged because you are wearing the ring I gave you. At least I think we are. Can you confirm that, miss?" Jason asks playfully.

"Oh, I don't know. This is kind of a cheap ring, so I am thinking this is probably not really an engagement ring but a ring a friend gives to a friend they don't really like all that much," Jeanette says, laughing playfully back.

She is thinking to herself just how much she loves this man and how much she hopes what she does for a living will not tear them apart.

Well, I am not going to think about it tonight, she thinks.

She is exactly where she wants to be, in his arms and falling asleep just like that.

"Good night, my sweet prince," she whispers to Jason as he starts to drift off.

Chapter Fifteen

As Trevor is getting ready to check in to his first day on the job as a real, full-fledged FBI field agent, he starts to get worried about how he will do. He left so much in the air when he left for Quantico. He is thinking to himself all the things he needs to get back in touch with.

First and foremost, the investigation into Christopher's murder. He never felt good about leaving without a resolution on that, but he knows that Jimmy had everything under control. Plus, this is a murder investigation. It won't be resolved in a couple of months. He can't put his life on hold while he waits for an outcome. Second, how could he turn such an opportunity down? He is so grateful for this chance, and he is going to make this the best decision ever. So first things first.

Greg is expecting him on time at the FBI field office on Fourth Street in DC. It will take him about thirty-five minutes to get there per GPS, so he wants to leave in plenty of time in order to get there early. He wants to be sure he can find where in the building he needs to go. Greg told him where that is, but it's a huge building. He has never been there before, so he doesn't want to leave anything to chance. He figures he will leave in a few minutes, which should give him plenty of time.

Rodney is doing rounds within the scope of his authority at the museum. One thing that no one knows is that he has always been the one to do rounds alone. Never has he done it with anyone on his staff. There is a very plausible reason for that. His rounds consist of what the museum considers high-value areas, the ones that have the most valuable displays. Now these displays have a great deal of electronic security on them, so no one can get near them without setting off all the alarms. He knows this as does every other security officer working there. So when Rodney does his rounds, it consists of those areas, but he doesn't do a very top-notch job of that. Knowing that it's so secure, he doesn't really do the best he should, especially as the security chief.

He detours to the customs arena. The customs arena is the area that is the final stop before everything goes out to the customs delivery teams on a scheduled pickup, just like there is a scheduled drop as well. There are several crates being shipped. In almost every shipment, there are at least thirty to forty crates going out at one time. This is good for Rodney because customs is not going to check all these crates to ensure they are what the manifest says is in the crates. What no one knows—and he has been getting away with this for almost five years now—is that Rodney and his partners have been shipping a drugstore of illegal drugs overseas every month for over five years since. It has been going great, and Rodney and his pals have gotten extremely rich in the process. He can't stop it, though, because it is shipping to the drug cartels in several countries. The historical museum ships to Mexico, Brazil, and several European and Asian countries. It's a process that has been perfected over the years and is now a well-oiled machine. Everything goes out like a regular shipment every month like clockwork. If this Harvey gets too nosy, he will have to die also.

Since this is not the first time he has killed to keep this secret, he is sure it will not be the last. For that matter, if Jimmy gets too nosy, he, too, will have to die. He doesn't think this will get that far. It was pure rotten luck that Jimmy saw the body in the setup area. He couldn't get the body out of there fast enough, and he couldn't say no to Jimmy because he would want to know why. So he had to go along with it and try to circumvent it the best he could. He wasn't counting on this Harvey cop though. He was asking far too many questions, and he was not sure Harvey was believing all the answers.

Trevor has made it to the FBI field office where his new career starts. He is really nervous as much as he is excited. Trevor is thinking that he has plenty of time to get to where he needs to in the building because he is incredibly early, but he doesn't want to be late and he wanted to have an opportunity to talk to Greg before he officially starts. He wants to sort of thank him for this incredible chance he has given him. The training was pretty grueling, but boy, he learned a lot, and he is grateful.

Trevor has gotten to the floor he is supposed to report to, and he sees Greg up ahead.

"Trevor? How the heck are you? I hear training went really well. In fact, the commander tells me you graduated at the top of your class. Nicely done. Congratulations." Greg reaches out to shake Trevor's hand.

Greg is more than pleased to hear about Trevor's success at Quantico.

"Thanks, Greg. Just blind luck, I guess."

"Oh, I doubt that was the case. I am just glad you are back because I have a case for you, and it's a big one. It actually involves the historical museum. But I am going to wait to tell you more until everyone gets here. Everyone should be here shortly. We are going to be combining our efforts with the Drug Enforcement Administration. The DEA."

As Greg says this to Trevor, the DEA agents start to filter in. As they do, Greg introduces them to Trevor as their newest agent.

"Now that everyone has been introduced, let's get started," Greg says as they all take seats in their conference room. "Okay, to get started, let me give you some background on what we are doing. First off, before I turn this over to the head of this task force at the DEA, let me say that we have been watching this for a while now. We are not entirely sure how they are doing this, but drugs have been filtering out of the museum on a fairly regular basis. From what we have been able to determine, this has been going on without suspicion for the past five years. That is how well this has been going for these—for lack of a better name—criminals.

"For that, I turn this meeting over to Dave Trenton. He has been following this the past few weeks, and we are ready now to start moving on this. Dave?" Greg turns this over to Dave Trenton to finish the briefing.

"Thanks, Greg. Before we begin, I want to congratulate Trevor for finishing at the top of his class at Quantico. Trevor, we are all proud of you and very happy you are part of this team."

Trevor nods and smiles as several members of the team shake his hands.

"So to get started, let me start by telling you that we have been getting reports from several law enforcement agencies around the globe about shipments of drugs that seem to be coming from the historical museum. Now we can't just rush in and bust everyone as much as I would like to because at this point, there is nothing to confirm that and we do not have a shred of evidence to support that. Because of this museum, we can't do a thing unless we have strong—real strong—evidence that supports this.

"Now currently, there is an investigation already under way at the museum because there was a murder there a few months ago. The person heading up that investigation goes by the name of Jimmy at the metro police department. The person murdered was a man named Christopher. He was brutally beaten and then stabbed to death for his troubles. I am not going to go over the investigation they are involved in because it's a separate issue. However, we can piggyback on their investigation, which will give us access to the museum and any information they have gathered to this point.

"One note, Christopher was a friend of Trevor's, and we are very sorry for your loss, Trevor, and we would certainly understand if you decided you didn't want to be a part of this," Dave says, looking toward Trevor.

"Thank you, Dave, but if it's just the same with you, I would like to be a part of this, and who knows? Maybe during this joint investigation, we will be able to find out who murdered Christopher. I would love to be the one to bust whomever that person is. Plus, Jimmy is a friend of mine. We went to college together many years ago. I think if I were a part of this investigation, I might be able to get more cooperation out of metro police because of our friendship. So I am on board all the way," Trevor says pretty much to the whole room but mostly to Dave.

"That is great, Trevor, and I was really hoping you would feel that way, but I wanted it to be your decision, not ours. I would like to say, though, if you feel at any point that it is getting too personal, then let me know and I will help you out the best way I can. Also, question for you, Trevor, has anyone at the historical museum seen you? I mean, you were friends with Christopher. Did anyone else happen to see you there while visiting Christopher, or did you never go there to see him?"

"No, I only saw him there once, and we never encountered anyone else while I was there. I was never there for more than a few minutes. The next thing I knew, Jimmy was telling me they found Christopher's body in the setup area down by the docks. So if we need to go undercover, I can do that without suspicion," Trevor states for all to hear.

"That sounds good, but I don't think putting someone undercover at the museum is the answer to this because if this operation has been going on for the past several years, they will not easily just bring someone new into it. We are going to have to think of another way to get our evidence. So I want ideas by noon tomorrow. We are going to have another meeting at noon, and I want some plausible ideas that we can explore. I need to talk to Greg about a few things, so the rest of you, stay put and start putting your heads together on how we can gather information and circumvent this alleged operation at this very big and important museum. Okay, everyone, dismissed. Greg? Give me a minute," Dave says over the heads of several of those in the room.

"Dave, what's up?" Greg shouts back over his shoulders.

"Let's go into your office," Dave says as he ushers Greg into his office and closes the door.

"Listen, I am really impressed with Trevor. His marks from Quantico were off the charts, and yet I am a little concerned about this connection he has with this case," Dave says with a little trepidation.

"Look, Trevor is a great guy and will be a great agent. His marks, as you say, tell us that. From what I know about him, and I confess it's not a lot, but his previous boss told some things about him that tell me how he will act in situations like this. I can tell you that he will be on this case whether we like it or not. He was a very good friend of this Christopher, and he wants to know why he died and who is responsible. Also, I am certain that regardless of what happens, he will be the professional we both believe him to be. I honestly don't think we have anything to worry about.

"One thing I really admire about him is, he is loyal to his friends and he is the type of person that already considers everyone in that room including you and me among them. I happen to know that he is going over to this Sheppard Security Services agency later today to help out a friend who he thinks is in danger, and he is bringing some of the guys with him to back him up so he knows the right thing to do, so I am sure he will make the right choices."

"Jeremy?" Jason calls out as he walks through the doors of the Sheppard Security Services company.

Jeremy's sister is sitting at her desk in the front lobby area of the office. Jeremy and Jason's offices are in the back section of the office.

"Jeremy!" Jason calls out again.

This time, Jeremy comes out from the back offices to see what all the fuss is all about.

"Jeremy, I need to see the books showing all of the finances. Every penny needs to be in there. It's time for me to make another deposit of my investment, and before I do, I want to see the books. The real books, Jeremy. Not the second set of books you have Marisol doctor for my benefit and whomever you are trying to fool with these fact books."

Marisol, Jeremy's sister, starts to get up with a stack of papers in her hand.

"Sit down, Marisol," Jason says. "Do not get up from that desk. If you want to get up, leave everything there. Take nothing with you. And then leave the building by way of the front door. Your choice but I want you where I can see you."

"Jason, what is this all about? We have been working together for the past several months without incident, so what is all this about?" Jeremy says with his hands in the air.

"I was checking out our bank accounts, Jeremy. Care to guess what I found? Well, actually, you don't have to guess. You know exactly what I found: serious discrepancies in deposits. We do not have nearly as much money as what we should have. Now I want to know where the rest of the money is, and I want to know now. The only document that should be able to tell me are the accounting books. So tell me, Marisol, Jeremy? How many sets of books are there?"

"Jason, I don't know what you are getting so upset about. The books are fine, and every penny has been accounted for."

"Show me," Jason says with his fists raised up shaking.

Jason does not like to be cheated on or taken advantage of. He knows there is something really fishy going on here with these books and the money for this business.

"Well, I tested you both. I knew that you both were involved. You, Marisol, are conducting creative bookkeeping for Jeremy. Before this, I wasn't able to prove it. Now I can. I earmarked several deposits that Marisol assumed came from you. These deposits were from several customers that mailed in their checks to us. I had the mailman deliver those checks directly to me without your knowledge, Jeremy. As half owner of this agency, you gave me that right. Didn't think I was sharp enough to figure this out, did you? I ran Donald Vernon's company for him for years. There are $120,000 missing from the deposits that Marisol sent in to the bank. The deposit complete was to be $280,000, but it was short by the $120,000. The books that Marisol handed me a few minutes ago show the full $280,000, but here is the bank deposit record of what was actually deposited. And this came from the bank: $160,000 was actually deposited. Where's the rest?"

Jason is ranting at this point. He is more than pissed about this. There is no way for Jeremy to explain this away. There is also, as he suspected, a second set of books.

"Well, Jeremy? What do you have to say about all this?" Jason asks.

"I am telling you that the bank made a mistake."

"Really? You're going to blame this on the bank? So let me get this straight. You are saying the bank made a $120,000 accounting error? Wow, that's good. Really good. You are stealing from the company and not just a small amount. You are into the felony-size theft. Anything you want to say before I call the police?"

Jason gives him one chance to come clean.

"You know, you are so right, Jason. I think it is time to come clean. You are so right. I am stealing like crazy from this company. I am living a millionaire lifestyle, thanks to this company. Happy? Now don't move a muscle because if you so much as flinch, I will shoot you where you stand," Jeremy says to Jason as he produces a Glock 45 and points it straight at him. "I have no issues about killing you right here and saying that it was a disgruntled employee."

"I see what you mean," says Jason as he puts his hands up so as not to make Jeremy nervous. "You know, Jeremy, since you are going to kill me anyway, why not, before you do, fill me in on what the plan here was. I mean, something went wrong here. Had to have. Somehow I don't think this gun was the plan. Or was it?"

Jason is surprisingly calm. What Jeremy does not know is that Jason invited Trevor to this little party of theirs. Trevor is quietly taping the whole conversation from the front door, and because Trevor is in Jeremy's blind spot, he can't easily see him. Trevor has his gun pointed straight at Jeremy in case he tries anything stupid like trying to just shoot Jason.

"No. I can tell you this was not supposed to be the plan, but you were too smart and you caught on way to soon. You were supposed to deposit your second investment check first. All right, so the plan was not supposed to go off like this, nor was it supposed to end up with you dying. But now you have to because there is no way otherwise. We were going to get away clean. We were just going to drain the accounts once we have as much as we can get in there at one time and also take the cash we have been tucking away. You weren't supposed to catch on to that. How did you, by the way? We had that hid pretty well, and everything we were telling you was plausible, right? I mean, you were buying this. So where did we go wrong?" Jeremy waves the gun in his direction.

Marisol is staying perfectly still. She tries to signal to Jeremy to let her get out of here.

"Okay, you want to know where you went wrong. I will tell you. You took way too much cash out without it being recorded. Didn't you think that I would be keeping somewhat of an eye on the money? You really didn't think I would just leave everything to your sister, did you? What kind of a partner would I be if I just took her word or yours? So that's it, huh? You are going to kill me, and then what? What is the new plan?" Jason asks, still with his arms up in the holdup position.

"Well, I don't know. Think we will just wing it and throw your dead body in the trunk. How about that?"

"Very nice, and then what? Throw my body out in the woods somewhere? Great plan," Jason says as his arms start to falter being in that position for so long. "Well, Jeremy, I hate to throw a monkey wrench into the plan, but take a look over there."

Jason points to the opening by the front door that was in Jeremy's blind spot.

"Did you get it all, Trevor?" Jason yells over to Trevor at the door.

Trevor has his gun pointed straight at Jeremy's chest. "Got it all. His full confession and his implication of everything little sister has been doing. They are both going to jail for a very long time. I wouldn't do anything stupid, Jeremy. You are well covered."

Jeremy is thinking he has a better shot than this kid by the door, so he shoots at Trevor. Trevor ducks, and Jeremy's bullet missed him completely. Trevor fires back at Jeremy, a direct hit in the middle of Jeremy's chest. Trevor was taught this was the best place to hit someone because they will live but be in a great deal of pain for a very long time.

Trevor races to Jeremy and kicks the gun from his side and tells Jason to grab Marisol and hold her. As he does, three other agents come running in to take charge of the scene. Trevor then rushes to Jason's side to make sure he is okay.

"Jason, you okay, bud?"

"Yeah, Trevor, thanks. You saved my ass. Boy, it really does come in handy to have a friend that is a federal agent. You really saved the day. There was no telling what that crook was going to do. But you are sure you got everything on tape?" Jason wipes his brow from sweating so much.

"The others will take it from here, Jason. There will be one hurdle to get over after this, and then you should be good. You will need to go before a judge and lobby to get control of the Sheppard Security Services agency while you work on your agency license as a single owner. You will have to tell them what we went through and why you are asking for control in the interim, which means if granted, the judge will give you permission to run the agency yourself without a license while you are obtaining one. Only a judge can sanction that. It shouldn't be an issue with all the corroborating evidence we have, plus I and my fellow agents involved will stand as witnesses for you, so it will just be a matter of formality. But the judge does have to pound his gavel and say yes."

Trevor explains this process to Jason as he cleans up himself, as well as the office.

"Okay, so right now I am good to run things until we go to court?" Jason asks.

"Yes, as partner in this business, you have the authority to take over until a judge gives their ruling. In the meantime, get started on the agency license paperwork. The sooner you get that submitted, the sooner you will have complete control over this place. Suffice it to say, Jason, there is no reason for a judge to deny you, so you just have to wait. You will be fine, and you will have this whole place to yourself legally before too long. So for that, congrats. Sorry it had to go this way for you to get it. By the way, sorry I didn't take you more seriously way back when you first told me your suspicions. It all worked out fortunately."

"Trevor, thank you so much for being here when I need you. That's what really counts. You believed me when you needed to, and you were there and saved my life. Jeremy's plan was to kill me. That's what his endgame was, so you being here stopped me from dying. You are a hero and my best friend."

"Let's get out of here."

Chapter Sixteen

"Hey, Trevor!" Jimmy yells from across the lawn as he parks his car. "Welcome home, my friend. I see you made it through training. I have a friend that was one of your training instructors. Did you really finish at the top of your class?" Jimmy approaches him, shaking his hand very enthusiastically.

"Guilty as charged," Trevor says as he escorts Jimmy into the house.

Jimmy is greeted by Jasmine, who apparently missed him. She jumps up to hug him as only dogs can do.

"Hey, girl. How's my sweetheart?" he says to Jasmine as he walks her into the living room as she is still hanging on to him.

"Looks like someone has missed you, Jimmy," Trevor says. He tells Jasmine, "That's enough."

Trevor says to Jimmy, "Well, I am glad to see you, Jimmy. I was going to call you if I hadn't heard from you before tomorrow."

"I was just giving you some breathing room to get reacclimated to being back home. After all, you were gone for twenty weeks. I just didn't want to run up on you as soon as you got home."

Jimmy fills Trevor in on where they are at in the investigation, and Trevor tells Jimmy about his first assignment.

"Wow, that's awesome, Trevor. That means now we really can help each other out on this investigation."

"Well, yes and no. You are more on the murder of Christopher, and I am on the drugs that seem to be flowing through the museum and have been for the past five years. No doubt, our investigations will coincide, but I want you to know that I am there to work with you on this murder if you need me because I am committed to getting to the bottom of Christopher's murder as much as I am in solving this drug case. I will share with you if you will share with me. I am not saying I'll hide anything from the FBI, but if it involves Christopher, will you promise me to share with me first?" Trevor asks Jimmy.

"Of course, I will. I will just give you advanced notice by a day, when I can?"

"That works for me. Since its your investigation on the metro side, that would not be an issue, but I don't want you to alienate the FBI and have them stop sharing with you. They know we are friends. They are fine with our friendship," Trevor says rather quietly as if there could be someone listening.

"Cool. Then we are set. What's the next step for you, boys?"

"Well, we are having another meeting tomorrow at noon, and we are supposed to come up with some alternatives to how we are going to learn what's going on in there without going undercover. Our head of this task force doesn't think going undercover will work. If they have been doing this process successfully for five years without fail and problems, they are never going ingratiate anyone new into their operation easily, so that was killed right away. Too risky. We did come up with some pretty good ideas that we will go over with Dave and Greg tomorrow. One of them was to actually open up every one of the crates they ship out of there. Well, we saw the inventory of what goes out of there on a very regular basis. It's staggering. Did you know that two to three times a week, over three hundred crates get shipped out of there? That's an average of six hundred crates a week.

"The problem with this scenario is, if we opened up every single crate, we would have to open them, inspect, and reclose them in a very short span of time. The thing is, we don't want to raise suspicions by opening the crates up at the museum or having the museum not close them so we can inspect them first because we want to let those running this drug operation to keep on running it until we are ready to grab them. We want them to think that it's business as usual.

Well, that's all I have for now on where we are going with this, other than to say we will probably have the crates opened up in another secured location so we can open them up without anyone seeing what we are doing. Once we decide exactly what we are going to do, we will need to get the cooperation of the museum in order for that part of it. Greg says the one thing we are going to prepare for is that there will be deadlines that will have to be met. Those will not be negotiable if we want them to continue to cooperate. So that will be a fine line."

Trevor wraps things up. He has caught up on where Jimmy is, and Jimmy has caught up on where the FBI and DEA task force is right now. Jimmy is happy to see Trevor back and taking such a take-charge attitude—a real difference from what he was like before he left. It seems Trevor has grown up a bit since he left for training. Jimmy is smiling approval.

"Okay, gotta go early morning tomorrow, and I suspect you do too," Jimmy says as he bolts out the door. "Good night, Trevor. Glad you're back, and I will see you tomorrow."

"Good night, Jimmy. Have a great night."

Jason walks into the Sheppard office the day after the incident where Jeremy wanted to kill him and said as much. Well, at least he is in a prison hospital room now, healing from Trevor's gunshot wounds. And that sister of his is sitting in a jail cell somewhere.

What a pair of crooks, Jason thinks. *I hope they get life.*

They won't, but he's hoping as he raises his coffee cup to the ceiling.

Now it's time to see how much damage there is here. His first stop is to the bank to see if there are hidden accounts somewhere that he can draw from. He might have to take out loans to salvage this place, but he doesn't want to do that if he won't be allowed to keep it. He has a long way to find that out.

Well, I guess one thing at a time, Jason thinks. *Let's just see where we stand.*

As he is thinking that, he is going through every drawer, cupboard, or cabinet in this building to see if he can find anything and hopefully have something to work with. He knows he is not completely broke because there is $160,000 that is in their bank account that he does know about. But he needs to pay bills too. Marisol probably didn't pay those either. He is going to literally have to go over everything and see what has or hasn't been paid and get what he can paid so he can keep the lights, phone, and such on.

For a business, $160,000 is not going to last long. He also has to look into the security guard schedules and who is maintaining those and what accounts they have beyond what he has been working with the past few months. Jeremy had his hands in a lot of the pie here, so now that it's all his to run, he needs to have a game plan and a team meeting of all the above security guard staffers and let them know what happened here yesterday. He has captains, lieutenants, and sergeants that have been pretty much running the day-to-day business for them. Some of them are loyal to Jeremy, but they might not be so much if they knew what happened. Jason has to be ready that some of them might leave. He will explain to them what happened, and all he can do is ask them to stay. If they still want to leave, there is nothing he can do to stop them.

Okay, so on to the business at hand, Jason thinks. *Where are we?*

"Okay, everyone, let's come to order," Dave says to all the agents sitting in the conference room, waiting for their noon meeting at their FBI field office.

"Before we begin," Greg says, "I want to congratulate Trevor, Brandon, Steve, and Austin for their efforts last night. I read your report. For those of you that don't know, these four went out to Maryland last night to rescue one of the partners of the Sheppard Security Services agency from his partner who was stealing untold huge sums of money from the company and then ended the criminal reign by trying to kill his partner. Trevor was able to disable the man, a Jeromy Blackstone, from his weapon after he shot at Trevor and his partner, a Jason Brandt was able to avoid getting hit, and Trevor shot him with non-life-threatening injuries. Way to hit the ground running, Trevor. Kudos to you all."

Greg wraps it up so Dave can start the meeting.

"Yes, awesome job and kudos from me as well. Trevor, I was told you were one to watch. I see why now." Dave grabs his notebook.

"Just part of the team, Dave. Glad I was able to help," Trevor says with all modesty.

"Okay, on to the business we are here to discuss. Have any of you or all of you come up with some ideas of how to inspect crates earmarked in or out of the museum without drawing suspicions?" Dave says to the group to no one in particular.

Branson, one of the new agents on the DEA team, puts up his hand to speak. "Dave, we have been brainstorming, and I think we have an idea. But we will need cooperation from the historical museum."

"Well, let's hear it and see if we can iron it out. If you all think this will be a good plan, let's talk about it."

A burly guy named Andrew says, "Well, what we were thinking is, if we could keep the illusion that one courier—the normal courier—picks all of the crates up as he usually does and takes the crates somewhere else so we can inspect them privately, we can put together a team of agents that can search the crates. Then once they are searched, we seal them back up and send them on their way. We would have to have quite a few agents or workers doing these inspections because there are like six hundred crates a week. Since we don't know when the drugs go out, we will have to search them all."

Dave sits and ponders this for a while before he speaks up. "Okay, I like it. It has possibilities to be sure. So we put a team of people together, and all they are looking for are drugs hidden in the shipments. This will work. Greg, we will leave it to you to talk to the museum. We know that they know there is a possibility that drugs are being run out of there. We know it's more than a possibility, but when we last spoke to the museum, they were not so much convinced. They don't think—no, they don't believe—it's possible for that to happen under their very noses and certainly not at the historical museum. After all, it's the historical museum. Those are their words, not mine. So, Greg, I will leave it to you to speak to them and as soon as possible. We need them to be on board with this. Then we need to speak to the courier company management and get them on board. We really can't approach them unless the museum is on board with it. Oh, Greg, if they hem and haw about it, tell them let us prove them right. If there is nothing going on, then no harm, no foul. Also, you can add that they certainly want drug trafficking stopped if it's there, right? Approach it like that if worst comes to worst.

"Okay, so we have a plan for part 1 of the process. Are drugs coming in and out of the historical museum? Now for part 2, once we prove that drugs are coming through there, how do we prove who is behind this?" Dave gets his second wind now. He exhales after spelling everything out for them based on their brainstorming.

Trevor raises his hand. "Dave, I have an idea. You know, nothing pisses off a drug dealer more than another drug dealer taking away business. What if we were to put another drug dealer on the streets? One of us. We get a backstop written for the agent who goes undercover, and he gets hidden really well behind his lieutenants and bodyguards and make it almost impossible for these drug dealers to find out who the top guy is but not impossible to find. We let him find our drug dealer when we are ready for him to. Play it up really well, and make it so whoever the drug dealer is that we are looking for will have to reveal himself eventually in order to save face. We start taking business away from them. That will really piss them off if we eat into their profits."

Again, Dave sits there just contemplating this latest idea. "Trevor, that is a brilliant idea. You are so right. Nothing will piss them off more if they lose money. Okay, put a plan together. I want everyone on this. This plan of Trevor's will work if we do it right. Greg, get Barb to start backstopping Trevor."

Barb is the admin assistant for Greg and his fellow managers and leads.

"Wait, Dave. Am I to understand that Trevor is going to be our drug dealer?" Greg says with a bit of concern.

"It's his idea, so yeah, he should be allowed to be the one doing it. Trevor, you are really new, and I do not want you to do this if you do not think you can do it or if you just don't think you are up to it. You tell us. Before he answers, I want to take a vote. Is there anyone that thinks this is a bad idea?"

Not one hand went up.

"Okay, it's up to you, Trevor. If you want to do this, then it's yours. We will backstop you, and we will get your crew together so you are well padded as far as coverage. After all, if you are to be the topman, you need to have plenty of lieutenants and soldiers in front of you. We start taking away their business on a consistent basis. I want this to be a quick operation, so we need to start digging into their business as soon as we are ready. The operation starts with getting the crates to an off-site location so we can search them. We will start taking smaller amounts of their drugs from the crates and then keep raising the stakes little by little. Every good drug dealer knows exactly what he has and how much each shipment is worth. We should start seeing action soon after we start.

"Now hear this. We do not want any—I repeat, any—chances of any of our people to get hurt or dead. So everybody protects everybody. I will be out and about, and so will Greg. All we need is to hear from Trevor. We haven't heard from you yet if this is something you think you can do." Dave points at Trevor.

"Absolutely, I am on board. I am up for this, and in fact, I am determined to do this," Trevor says with more determination than he intended.

"Okay, so Trevor is on board," Greg says. "Great. I have just been looking at this plan and how best Dave and I can figure in without being too obvious. We will each set up a cutting and distribution center on different sides of town. These will be safe places for you to go if you need us. What Dave said goes double for me. Watch your backs and one another. It will take a few days to get everything set up. We have two warehouses that we have used for training in the past. There are no ties to DEA or FBI. They are completely neutral buildings, and no one would ever know what they were ever used for. So we are safe. The one on the east side is closest to the historical museum where the customs shipments are kept before they are picked up, so we can use that as the place where we set up the operation to inspect every shipment." Greg heads toward the door. "I need to get Barb to start working on Trevor's backstop, and Amanda, our DEA Secretary will start working on pulling in people to inspect the crates. Dave and I will start getting prepared for Trevor's coming-out party."

"We figure we will need at least two lieutenants and five or six soldiers to protect Trevor," Dave says. "We need to show the image of protection for him, so anyone that would like to volunteer, let me or Greg know and we will get you backstopped as well."

Greg starts writing out notes to himself on what he needs to do now. First stop is going to be the historical museum. *If they don't go along,* Greg thinks, *we are dead in the water before we get started.*

"Dave will go talk to the courier management and get them on board," Greg says. "We just need them to bring the crates to our warehouse first so we can inspect them."

Greg continues to write instructions to himself. He finds he doesn't forget anything if he writes everything down.

Oh yes, need to know how much time we have with the crates after they are dropped off to the warehouse, Dave thinks. *God, I hope we get enough time to properly inspect them.* He writes down.

Okay, off to the museum with fingers crossed.

Greg has asked to speak to the director, Bartholomew Alexander, at the museum.

The director's office is the best place to start. According to Mr. Alexander's office in Maryland, they might have to call for an emergency board session to approve or disapprove this plan of ours. That could take some time, but in the meantime, we can work out all of the other details. Mr. Alexander's office seemed concerned that there might be a drug trafficking problem at their museum. We were told his office will assist where they can. Not all members will be able to attend, but if they have a majority, they would certainly be able to get an approval. That's what Greg is hoping for anyway. With it being the historical museum, it's hard to get one approval when there are mostly board committees that make the decisions, but we will see what we can do. I'll meet with them the day after tomorrow.

"Harvey, can you come here a minute? I have some information to share that we need to prepare for and get ready for," Jimmy says to Harvey. "We are about to get help on this investigation. Turns out the FBI and the DEA are now interested in this case because it's not just about Christopher's death anymore. It's now about what's going on in the museum that has surfaced a lot of interest and concern. There is a suspected drug operation going on in there. Apparently, millions of dollars' worth of drugs are going in and out of this place. Someone is using the historical museum as a drug center for drug dealers all over the world. I can see how easy that would be to do. Think about it, there is no one person watching the store. Everything at the museum is decided through committees."

"Well, that seems to be on track with what I have been saying then," Harvey responds back. "Who else but a bigwig in security would be able to pull something like this off? That makes me think even more now that it's this guy Rodney."

"I have to agree with you more now than before. I was on board with your suspicions before because I trust your instincts, but now with this new information, he is the perfect person to pull something like this off," Jimmy says.

"My thoughts exactly. So what's the plan then?" Harvey says.

"Well, we are going to partner up with the FBI in the part that involves them. The murder is still all ours, but they are pretty sure that this is all tied in together. We solve the drug crime, the who and what of that, and we will more than likely also solve who murdered Christopher."

As the phone on his desk rings, Dave runs over from across the room to answer it. "Hello, this is Dave. How can I help you?"

"Dave, this is Brett from the Washington Customs Service. I am returning your call. How can I help you?" Brett responds in kind.

"Well, we have a few issues at the historical museum that we need your cooperation with."

As Dave fills Brett in with what they are looking for, Brett is listening intently.

When Dave is done telling him what they were looking for, Brett says, "We are certainly happy to work with you on this. One thing I want you to be sure you know is the crates are all on deadlines. Those deadlines are tighter with regard to the historical museum because there is not as much individual crate inspection because of who they are. So to summarize, just to be sure I have it right on what you are looking for is, we pick up the crates like normal so as not to arouse suspicion. And then we bring these crates to this warehouse of yours, and we leave them there for your people to search every crate. Once they are done searching the crates, we come back and pick them up and take them to their destination as normal.

"So you are aware you will only have those crates in your warehouse for three days. That is the absolute most we can give you. If the crates are going by air, then you have a little more time. But most of the crates are going by ship. That's where the three days max come in. The ships can only stay in port a certain amount of time. Tell me one thing though. If your people do find drugs in these crates, then what? Are they going to send them out anyway?"

"Very good question. We are going to take half of the total stash of drugs and send the rest out tagged. The idea is twofold. We are going to set up our own drug dealer trafficking network that will rival whomever is dealing at the museum. The idea will be to get those dealing at the museum to notice and want to find out where their drugs are and who took them. That's where our drug network comes into play. We start getting our dealers into the mix and involved more and more. We want to piss off these dealers to the point they come after our guys. I don't like the idea of sending the drugs we find—even some of them—out to their initial destination, but we got our director's approval on that, so we can smoke this whole network out and put a stop to this all in one fell swoop. All we need from your guys is just deliver the crates, and we will let you know once they are ready to go. I promise we will keep it to the three days. We will just put more people on it.

"One last thing I need from you. An approximate number of crates each day or week. If you can provide that, we can get enough people opening them up and sealing them again. I have a guy in mind that is great at this kind of organization. So any more questions I can answer or are you pretty caught up on what we need?" Dave starts to get up as to end this call.

"Yeah, I got it. We will definitely work with you on this. If someone is really doing what you say, we need to put a stop to it. I'm good, Dave. Thanks."

"Thank you, Brett. We will be in touch as soon as we are ready. Shouldn't be more than a couple of days. Until then, business as usual, okay?"

"You got it. I will wait to hear from you. Talk to you soon," Bret says as he hangs up.

Awesome, Dave is thinking. *Part 1 is set.*

Chapter Seventeen

"Hey, Jason. How are you doing today, my darling? I hope you are recuperating from that horrible ordeal that awful man Jeremy put you through," Jeanette says with sweet compassion in her voice as the phone rings.

Wow, what a great lady, Jason thinks. *I can't believe I am so lucky. I get to marry that amazing woman.*

"I'm fine," Jason says. "No worse for wear. I am just about done here. Would you like to go out for a drink or maybe some dinner? I think we need to talk about this wedding that I seem to be involved in. Not sure why but I seem to think I should know more about this person that is getting married," Jason says jokingly. He wants her to always feel loved and needed.

We are going to have a great life together, Jason thinks. *Now I need to talk her into a wedding not too far down the road.*

"I would love to go out with you tonight. You need a break from all the action. Tonight will be my treat too. You always buy. I want tonight to be from me," Jeanette says with all the love in her heart.

Jason arrives to pick up Jeanette, and she jumps in his arms and gives him a great big kiss.

"Hi, sweetheart. It appears you might have missed me," he says playfully.

"I did, and I am so glad you are all right. Are you ready to go? I am starved. By the way, Jason, do you think you can stay overnight tonight? I was thinking of me for dessert. Unless you don't want any of this." She flaunts her big breasts and thrusts her crotch in his direction. She is pretty sure he got her message. She wasn't all that subtle.

He laughs and says, "A well-rounded meal should always include a dessert."

Jeanette snickers and grabs her jacket as they head out the door.

"I think we should decide on a date for our wedding and who is going to be in it," Jason says as he pulls his car out of the driveway.

"I was thinking it should be more sooner than later," Jeanette says, now with a more serious look on her face. "I assume you will have Trevor as your best man. Do you think we need any more than one on each side?"

"I will definitely have Trevor, but I don't think we need to have more than one for each of us. We should make it a casual gathering instead of a stuffy formal affair. What do you think about that?"

"I like it," Jeanette says. "There is one thing that I do want though, a formal gown for me and a tux for you. I just have always dreamed of that for a wedding and wanted to have that for us and at least our maid of honor and Best man."

"Speaking of which, do you have someone in mind for your maid of honor? I mean, you have never really spoken of anyone that you were particularly close to, so I just wondered. Do you have any family or close friends? You really have not told me much about your private life other than things in the moment. I feel embarrassed to say I don't know all that much about you and who you are."

"There is not all that much to tell," Jeanette says. "I can tell you that I have one sister who lives in Maryland. She has a husband and two children. Girls. I would have her as my maid of honor. She is thrilled for us and can't wait to meet you. I have told her all about you, how handsome you are, and that you own your own business and stuff like that."

"What is your sister's name?" Jason asks.

"Bernadette. And her husband is Derek. Her girls are three and eight, and their names are Stephanie and Kaitlyn. They own a house in the Garrett Park district near a beautiful park where the girls spend a lot of time at. Not sure what else I can tell you. I lead a very boring life working for a customer service agency. My sister does not work.

Derek makes enough money, so she doesn't need to work. She is a stay-at-home mom. How about you? The only thing I know about you is your relationship with Trevor. You don't talk about anyone else. I don't even know if you have any other friends. I know where you work, and with some luck, you will end up owning the whole place before too long. Other than that, I know nothing else about you."

"There is not a lot to tell. I had a pretty rough childhood. My mom loved me to be sure, and I loved her. But have you ever heard the phrase 'Sometimes love just isn't enough'? Well, that was really true with my mom. She also loved her new husband and couldn't say no when he wanted me out of the house, so I got kicked out to appease her husband. I lived on the streets for quite a while after that, stealing food so I could eat. It was not a great upbringing in my teens. I was only sixteen at the time. The good news is, we have had a great relationship after she got rid of that husband of hers. She finally realized that she wasn't doing right for me and told her husband to go to hell. I have had mostly security jobs since I have been working. Mostly stuff in department stores as loss prevention. Then I got a job with a security company that was going great for five years, and that finally ended too. That brings us to when I met you, and the rest, as they say, is history. So tell me, where would you like to go on a honeymoon? Since I pretty much am in charge now, I can take time off if I need to."

"Well, I think we should get married sooner than later, and I think we need to hold off on a honeymoon for a while until your stuff with Sheppard gets settled. Didn't you say you have a hearing coming up in the next month or so to determine if a judge will let you continue to run things while you obtain a license? I think you need to concentrate on that for now. We can get married in the meantime, but let's do a honeymoon later. We can talk about it."

"Okay, what about a wedding in two months?" Jason says. "It's June now, so why not August? Will that work for you? I will make sure Trevor is available for that. I picked the month. Now you pick the day. Make it a Saturday, please." Jason says while holding her tightly and hugging her tightly.

"Greg," Amanda says from across the room as she approaches where Greg and Dave are standing and talking about this process. Amanda is the DEA Secretary, admin assistant, and as she puts it, chief cook and bottle washer. As she approaches them, she says to Greg, "Well, I have rounded up 135 agents and employees of the DEA and FBI combined. Everyone is willing to help."

"Great, okay," Greg says. "I have a meeting with the committee at the museum later today. I am sure they will be on board with this. I mean, why wouldn't they?"

"Okay, so, Amanda, have everyone report to the warehouse on New York Avenue and Florida in the Eckington area," Dave says. "The warehouse is only about seven minutes from here. Get everyone there tomorrow morning by 8:00 a.m., and Greg and I will address them and let them know what we need. We are going to have to wing it to start off with, so we will need some of them to help get things set up. Once I get the approval from the historical museum today, assuming I do, then I will let the Customs Service know to start dropping the crates off. Hopefully, I will have all the information I need by tomorrow morning. Like I said, have everyone there in the morning, eight a.m."

"Thanks, Amanda. Great job getting so many people so quickly and on such short notice," Greg says. "Okay, next step." Greg shouts out for Barb, "Barb! Where are you, Barb?"

"Here I am. I am still working on Trevor's backstop. I will have it done before morning. Trevor? Any thoughts on a name you would like?" Barb says to Trevor. "It would need to be a real drug dealer's name."

"Gosh, I don't know. Anyone have any ideas?"

Andrew pipes up again. "I have an idea. How about Carlos Ross. Carlos is a great drug dealer name, if you think about it. What do you think, Trevor?"

"I like it," Trevor says. "It's a good solid name for a drug dealer. Greg, Dave? What do you guys think? We need it to work, so if you don't think it will, tell us and we will come up with other ideas."

As Greg is sitting, thinking about this and all the other things that they have to get ready for, he nods in agreement. "Dave? What do you think?"

"I like it," Dave says. "Okay, so, Barb, let's go with it. We need Trevor's backstop to go out at least eight to ten years. He is supposed to be as much of a scum as the dealers we are trying to put out of business."

"No problem. I will have this all done by morning. So, Trevor, check in with me in the morning, and I will give you all you need. We are also putting you up in a rather questionable hotel that has been closed now for over a year. We are going to reopen it and put our people in there so you will be well protected. Who will be your crew? The ones protecting you. Any volunteers? Before anyone raises hands on this, just so you know, you will be on the front lines protecting Trevor or rather Carlos. That's why I want volunteers. I would say at least three lieutenants and four bodyguards. That should keep him plenty covered. We will follow Trevor's plan. We will let his identity be known only when we are ready for it to be. In the meantime, I will set up a cutting and distribution hub on one side of town, and Dave will set up the other. We will need agents for both of these operations. So let's go, everyone. Volunteers."

Immediately, Brandon, Steve, and Austin, the guys from last night that helped Trevor with Jason's situation, all put up their hands without hesitation.

"Speaking for the three of us, we would like to be Trevor's or rather Carlos's lieutenants," Steve says on behalf for them all. "We all feel we work good together, and we would like to continue working with him. That is, if Trevor will have us."

"I would be honored to have you on my team," Trevor says as he walks over and shakes all their hands. They kind of all hug in a "we are a team" embrace.

"Awesome. I can't be happier that you will all be working together again. Now we need some bodyguards to surround the four of them and keep them out of the limelight. How about some volunteers for that?" Greg says to the group.

All of a sudden, eight hands go up, and Dave pipes up. "Okay, great. We will use four of you as Trevor's bodyguards, and the rest of you will divide up and work in the cutting and distribution hubs. We should have more than just two extras in each. Greg and I will also be in these hubs, but I would prefer at least a couple more per hub. Anyone else want to volunteer? If not, I will just pick two more per hub. These hubs will not be dangerous. They will just be where we take the drugs after we take them from the crates. So we aren't really cutting and distributing drugs out of here. We are just storing them out of sight."

They get several more volunteers raising hands now.

"Okay, it looks like we have enough for the entire operation now. Perfect. Trevor, Steve, Austin, and Brandon, there is a makeup artist waiting for you upstairs to turn you into the look of drug dealers. Okay, everyone, from here on, Trevor is now Carlos until this operation is over, and we have everyone involved in custody. We are after the top of the food chain, so that's the prize. Let's go get this started. Good luck to us all."

Jeanette and Jason finish dinner and head for her house. Jason likes staying at her house. Although she rents, it's a better place for them to live after they get married, at least in his opinion. But he owns his house, and it is a very nice and comfortable house. He has lived there for a very long time. He has good credit, so maybe what they should do is sell his house and get rid of her rental and get a house that is theirs.

"So, Jeanette," Jason says after several minutes of silence. "A penny for your thoughts. You have been quiet. What you thinking about?"

"Oh, I don't know. Just happy and thinking I can't wait until we get married. I think we are going to have an incredible life," Jeanette says in a very, almost barely audible voice.

"Well, I was thinking you have a house you rent. I have a house I own. We definitely need to get rid of your rental and have you move into my house. How does that sound to you?" He was going to wait until they got to her house, but it seems too quiet in the car, so he decides to bring it up now, a discussion they can have now in the car and continue after they get home.

"Well, it makes good sense to have me move into your house. I don't own this house, so it will be easy to give it up. My lease is up in three months anyway. That's one of the reasons I was thinking ahead that we should get married sooner than later. I have been thinking on the same lines as you. I should move into your house after we get married. I can start staying over there more and more. It's not that we haven't spent several nights together already. I can start moving my stuff over a little at a time, if that works for you. I don't want to rush you."

"No, that's perfect. I was thinking the same. When we are ready to get the furniture, I will get Trevor to help out, and we can move my living room furniture to the family room in the basement. There isn't anything there right now. We move your furniture into the living room because your furniture is nicer than mine. As for everything else, we can slowly get your stuff moved. So we are agreed then. August. Two months and we get married. Pick a date, and I will let Trevor know. He is really busy right now with this big case they are working on. I want to give him plenty of time. And definitely plenty of advanced notice."

They approach her driveway. They walk into the house without saying another word. When they get inside, Jeanette is like a mad woman. She goes at Jason like he is the after-dinner treat and rips off his clothes and starts caressing him all over his body, especially his crotch area. She can feel the hardness down there, and she wants him so much right now. She tears his belt off him like she is on a mission. And boy, is she on a mission. She can't wait to get into the bedroom. She takes him right there in the front room. Jason grabs some pillows off the couch and puts them under his head since she is riding him and practically raping him on the floor inches from the front door. She is jumping all over the place as she makes love to him. He turns her over and is now on top of her as he is plunging into her.

When they are both spent, they just lay on the floor for a while, catching their breath. Jason just starts to smile and says, "So thought of a date yet? We need to get a firm date so we can book a party somewhere."

Jeanette starts to laugh. "Really, after what we just did, that's the first thing you think about? Wow, was I that uninteresting?"

"No, honey, not at all. I just have all this stuff on my mind, and I know that if I get too wrapped up in recovering from Jeremy at Sheppard, I will overlook some things about our wedding. I don't want that to happen. It's too important to me," Jason says softly as he puts her hand on his now limp member.

"Don't worry, baby. I will take care of the arrangements. I know you have way too many things to worry about right now. If you think we should wait, we can wait until things settle down a bit. I am okay with that."

"I know you are, but no, I do not want to wait any longer. Make your arrangements, and let's get married. I don't need a big wedding. Just marrying you is good enough. Your sister and Trevor, who by the way is like a brother to me, and anyone else you would like to join us. Do you have anyone in mind, or is it just going to be the four of us?"

"Well, definitely Bernadette's family will be there, and you should have your family there besides Trevor."

"I will invite my mom, as well as a couple of friends I have that have been important in my life for a number of years. Just people I know from the bar and previous jobs I have had. I will let you know. Were you thinking of invitations or just letting people know and personally inviting them to the wedding? I think our favorite bar would probably let us host it there."

The Madhatter is a place Jason and Trevor have been going to for years. Now it seems it's also a favorite place for Jason and Jeanette to go to as well. They seem to know quite a few people there.

"I will talk to Richard, the owner, and see if he would let us host it there. I am certain he will. I'm just not sure what he would charge us for the room. Anyway, I will talk to him in the next day or so." Jason yawns.

"You look tired, Jason. Why don't we go to bed?" Jeanette says while trying to soothe him a little. "I know you are busy at work and are spending a lot of time trying to iron everything out and getting yourself back on an even plain. You will get there."

She truly wants him to succeed. He has been worried about this hearing that is coming up in a couple of months. He's not sure what he needs to do to prepare for it, but he is gathering as much evidence as he can on all the things Jeremy did. He has the police report, as well as the FBI report of the night he was shot and what all transpired during all that. According to what Trevor is saying, he should be fine. Trevor will be there along with his partners that helped him that night, and they will all stand up and back Jason up.

Well, nothing I can do tonight, Jason thinks as he starts to get sleepy and begins to fall asleep.

And Jeanette watches him for a few minutes until she decides to just lay her head on his shoulder and fall asleep too. After all, tomorrow is another day.

Chapter Eighteen

"Dave?" Greg exclaims as he is walking through the door. "I just got approval from the historical museum. They wanted us to know that they don't believe that this is going on at the museum, but since there are several museums and they admit they don't have a watchful eye on all of them, they are willing to admit that anything is possible. Either way, we have their approval to do what we need to. They will conduct business like normal so as not to raise any suspicions.

"On the way here, I spoke to Brett from the Washington Customs Service, and he is going to start dropping their first shipment tomorrow morning. He did say that tomorrow should be a relatively light day. They are only expecting about thirty crates tomorrow, but it will double the next day. He will try to keep us informed if they know the number of crates ahead of time. Most days, they don't know. So, Amanda, I need everyone there in the morning, eight a.m. sharp."

"They will all be there," Amanda says from across the room. "I have several of the guys coming in earlier to help set things up, so when the crates arrive, we will be ready. We are going to make it as easy as we can. Question for you two though." Amanda walks in the direction of Greg and Dave. She is someone who is very methodical, the perfect person to head this part of the project. She will keep things moving and get these crates in and out as fast as possible. "When we find drugs, what do you want us to do with them? Is there like a holding place or bin or something you want us to put them in?"

"Yes, Amanda, they should already be at the warehouse for you. Now what we want is for only part of the whole taken out of there. So when you find drugs in a crate, take out half of what is in there and leave the rest. Reseal the crate, and have it moved to the pickup area for the customs service to pick up again. Okay, one last thing," Greg says for all to hear. "It will be several days before these drug dealers get wind that half their stash is missing. I have already put two agents on each customs courier in case they think the courier is who took their drugs. When they find out from their dealers around the globe as they start getting their shipments, they are going to hear really fast that drugs are missing. The dealers being shipped to will want answers from their connection at the historical museum. They will not have answers but will try to get them. We need to be on our toes when that happens."

"Barb, what's Trevor's status? Is he ready to go?" Dave asks.

"He is all set. Carlos is ready to start his new career," Barb states.

"Great," Dave says. "Sounds like we are ready to get this party started. Okay, Trevor, you will be at the warehouse closest to the historical museum for now. Since it will be a few days before you are discovered, we need you to hang out there for now. Brett from the customs service will have the first shipment there by eight thirty a.m., he figures. They pick up the crates at eight a.m. He says it will take them about a half hour to load up the crates and drop them off at the warehouse."

"Be ready, everyone," Greg says. "Tomorrow starts our sting operation. Everyone, go home and get some sleep. We start this plan in the morning, and I want everyone rested. Good night." Greg walks into his office to close it up and do the same thing himself.

"Good night, everyone," Dave says as he also walks out the door to do the same.

"Harvey, you got a minute?" Jimmy asks.

"Sure thing. What's up?" Harvey responds.

"Well, I heard from Greg at the FBI about their plan for the drug part of this operation. Greg has asked us to pause our investigation for now on anything that has any of us going to the museum. No one from this department is to go anywhere near the museum. They are afraid that it will draw suspicion on everyone involved in this drug sting that is starting tomorrow. They don't want any unnecessary attention drawn on them while they try to catch these guys. Greg assures me that during this operation or rather before this operation is completed, we—or they—will have the Christopher murder solved. It's all tied together, and when one is solved, they will both be solved. So we will follow the FBI and DEA directive and stay away from this investigation.

"Oh, and he did say that they will let us in on the kill when the time comes. There is a big operation going on here and has for at least five years that they are sure of. Maybe longer. Either way, they will let us in on the final takedown if they can. They are certain the drug dealers that are running this operation will eventually have to reveal themselves when they start losing product. If the dealers that receive the goods around the globe start getting half of what they are expecting, they will come after those running things here. When they do, FBI, DEA, and we will be ready. It will be the biggest bust this city has seen once it's all over."

"Do you really have to go Jason? It's so early," Jeanette says as she walks with Jason to the front door.

"I have to leave early. I have to go home and shower, get dressed in a suit, and start visiting clients. I am going out with the operations manager today. He is going to acclimate me to the operation and introduce me to some of the higher-end customers that we need to pay the most attention to. Also, he is going to go over the schedule with me so I know where everyone is working. He wants me to have the opportunity to change things up if I wanted to. I have not really gotten to know the operations manager all that much because Jeremy was really good about keeping our officers out of my reach. I think he was afraid I was going to learn things he didn't want me to learn. But now I need to know.

"This operations manager, a man named Lester, was loyal to Jeremy, so it might be hard to get him to cooperate fully with me. I haven't really filled him in yet as to what happened, so I think—or rather I hope—once I tell him what he did, he will switch his loyalty to me and help me get this company back on track. I don't have a bookkeeper now, so I need to figure that out today because the employees don't care what the troubles of the company are. They are going to want to get paid. That is definitely something I can understand, so I have to figure that out today because payday is on Friday, and I have no idea who is going to do the payroll now. Just one of many issues I have to resolve as quickly as I can. I will probably be hiring a temp service to do the payroll. That will put a Band-Aid on that issue for now. But I have to get them into the office working on this today.

"As you can see, it seems everything is going to have to happen today. Well, this is my problem. I don't need to burden you with any of this. I have to go. I do love you, Jeanette. I want to spend the rest of my life with you." Jason gives her a very passionate kiss.

"You go do what you have to, and I will talk to you later. I love you too, mister. You try to have a good day today. Bye!"

"Bye," Jason says as he walks to his car.

Jason gets to his office around 8:00 a.m. and ends up meeting Lester. He was also thinking that he needed to get here early too. As Jason greets him, he shakes his hand.

"How are you, Lester?" Jason says to him as he sits down at a desk across Lester. "Listen, Lester. I know you are loyal to Jeremy, but I need you to understand everything that went on here the other day."

As Jason explains to Lester all that transpired the other day, Lester is just holding his head down in total disbelief.

"Oh my god, he shot at you?" Lester exclaims, completely blown away by all this.

"He did, and it's a good thing I had my FBI friend here as a backup in case things got out of hand as they did. He recorded everything that Jeremy said, and just so you know, he had everyone fooled. He admitted to everything because he expected the day to end with him killing me. So he was not worried about telling me anything because I was supposed to be taking all that to my grave. I will tell you that my friend Trevor from the FBI did end up shooting Jeremy but with non-life-threatening injuries. We both wanted him going to jail, not a grave. That was never in the plan, but Trevor knew there was a possibility he would have to shoot him, and as it turned out, he did but not until after he shot at us. So all this being said, how do you feel about continuing your employment here? I would really like you to stay."

Jason reaches his hand out. He is hoping Lester will shake his hand in agreement to stay.

"I would definitely like to stay, and I am so sorry he did all that to you. I guess I really misjudged him. Well, you have my loyalty, Jason. Whatever I can do to help you in getting this company back on track and back where it should be, I will be there for you," Lester says to Jason as he stands up, shaking his hand.

"Thank you, Lester. Now let's see how much damage he caused. Will you see about getting a temp service in here to do payroll, unless you can do it or we have someone already working here that can."

"Yeah, I don't know anyone that can jump into that role that already works here. Let me see what I can do to find a temp service that specializes in that. I can give them all they need to do the payroll. I just can't do it myself. I can pull up all the current records on everyone that works here. So as long as I can give that to the payroll company, we should be okay." Lester starts searching the internet for a good reputable company that can do that right away.

"Thanks, Lester. I appreciate you working with me on this. Let's get to work."

Amanda walks into the warehouse on New York Avenue to a crowd of employees already getting things ready for their first shipment of crates. They have tables set up, and the bins are already on the tables, waiting for the drugs.

"Now this is what I call organization!" Amanda exclaims.

"Okay, it's about eight fifteen," Dave says. "We should see our first shipment in a few minutes. George, one thing I wanted to see on these crates is if there is anything distinctive on the crate that would tell the drug dealers on the receiving end that the drugs are in this crate. It might make this go faster if we had a clue as to which crates we can find the drugs."

George is the one person who organized this warehouse for the arrival of the crates. He has been with the DEA for twenty-four years and is considered one of the best investigators in the department, but in all his years, he has never wanted that. He works in the office working with the teams on various projects. When they need a fresh pair of eyes, they come to him. He has been offered so much more he just won't take it.

"George, I need one more thing from you," Dave says to him as he hands him a stack of papers showing where everything should be. "I need this warehouse to look like a real customs depot where they bring crates and process them through for anyone who is sending packages over the borders, specifically the historical museum. Okay, so I need you to research where they take their customs shipments for processing and duplicate that place with our warehouse. Brett from the Washington Customs Service has agreed to help in any way he can. Use him to get it up and looking legit inside a day. This whole process has gone up fast, so we don't want to miss a step or make a mistake. The stakes are way too high." Dave inspects what they have done. "Oh, and lock this place down. I want it impossible for anyone to get in here and see what we are doing." Dave starts calling Greg.

"Greg speaking."

"Greg, Dave. I wanted to bring you up to speed on where we are right now. The warehouse is set up and almost ready. George is going to make this warehouse look like the same building the Washington Customs Service uses. Brett is going to help him so they can get it done fast. How are things on your end?"

"We are ready here also. Trevor, or rather Carlos, is ready to take on his role in this. We have been circulating rumors around town to our snitches that there is a new drug dealer that has moved into town from the West Coast and has already taken on a lot of action here in DC. The rumor says he only deals in large quantities of heroin because that's what this dealer at the museum is dealing in. That should get their dander up a little. We are ready for this party to start. How far are we from the first shipment of crates?"

"We are only minutes away," Dave says. "First shipment should be here in a few minutes. It's already on its way. I figure we are safe for the next few days until the shipments start arriving to their destinations. We are also looking for ways to speed up the process over here. The way I figure it, there is a marking of some kind on the crates that no one else would pay attention to, but the drug dealers receiving the drugs know which crates have the drugs. Has to be. There are so many crates. They are not going to open them all. My thoughts on this are that at the receiving location, the drugs are being managed by someone that is in place in a receiving dock or receiving building or somewhere that puts shipments aside for only certain people to uncrate and distribute contents. And that person is working for these drug dealers here. They were put there, perhaps a long time ago.

"Now if we could circumvent this entire operation, we might be able to grab everyone. We would just need to know where they are being shipped to, and Brett can help us there. If we are lucky, they are not going to too many destinations. One thing I am completely sure of is, these shipments are regular. When these shipments go out of here, they are going to the same locations every month or even every week."

"Okay, I will get Barb to start putting a spreadsheet together as we learn of delivery locations. Once we repackage the remaining drugs per crate, we will have someone capture their destinations and see if there is a pattern." Greg writes himself some notes.

"This is going to be huge if we can get the other municipalities involved and swoop in and grab everyone," Dave adds. "That would be amazing."

"I will give Jimmy a call over at the police department and have him do the rundowns on the destinations as we get them," Greg says. "We can send them to his team to locate once we have a destination. Have him and his team reach out to the locals and have them stand by until we are ready. We do need to time this just right. We do not want the locals jumping the gun. That will blow everything."

"Agreed. I will leave that to you. Make sure you make it clear to him what our endgame is here. Make sure he is very clear on what the prize here is."

"Jason, sweet Jason. Could we get married a month earlier?" Jeanette asks Jason. "Say July instead of August? The reason I ask is because Bernadette isn't going to be available for most of the month of August because of stuff going on in the kid's schools. She just said it would be a whole lot easier if we could do it in July instead. Since we aren't really planning a specific reception and this is more of 'get married and then have a party at the local hangout,' I didn't think that would be an issue. What do you think?"

"I don't see a problem, but I have to check with Trevor to make sure it's going to be okay with him. He is involved in this big drug case right now, and I want to make sure he can get away. I will check in with him and let you know. Did you have a date in July you were looking at?" Jason asks.

"Yes, as a matter of fact, I did. I was thinking July 25. That is like the third Saturday in the month. It still gives us time, as well as Trevor and most of the other guests we may want to invite. But for Trevor, if he has enough advanced notice, it may be easier for him. Anyway, why don't you check it out with Trevor and let me know? My sister would like to see us get married at her church since we are not looking at anyone in particular. The only thing I don't like about that is if we have it there, her church is in Maryland, so it's quite a distance from the Madhatter. I still think that's the best place to have the party. People know us there. Well, let me work out the details with Bernadette, and I will let you get back to work."

"That's okay, honey. I could use the distraction. I will leave the details in your hands, and all I need to know is when to show up and where. By the way, I totally agree with you on the tuxedos and evening gowns so we feel like we are getting married, and besides, I want to give you that fairy-tale wedding you always wanted, let you look like a princess. Anyway, gotta run. Love you. Bye." Jason hangs up.

Chapter Nineteen

"Amanda, there is a guy named Rusty here to see you," George says from across the room.

"Rusty, I'm Amanda. You got some crates for us?" Amanda says, looking at the manifest.

"Yeah, got some crates to drop off for you. About thirty crates today. Where do you want them?" Rusty asks.

"Here, stack them up over here. We will take it from here. If you tell Brett to have someone back here tonight around six p.m., we can have them ready for you," Amanda says as she points to the open space they set aside for them.

"Great, that will probably be me," Rusty says. "That would be my last run of the night. It looks as though I will be your driver for most of the crates during the week. We don't have crates to pick up on Thursdays, but there should be crates the rest of the week. Also, Brett wanted me to tell you that this will probably be the smallest delivery you will see. We just didn't have that many on a Monday this week, but we usually do."

"Okay, great," Amanda says. "Well, we will do what we can to get them done in as quick a time as we can."

"Well, I better get them unloaded off the truck," Rusty says as he lowers the liftgate on the back of the truck.

"Dave, the first shipment of crates is here!" Amanda shouts from across the room as she starts walking toward him. "I will get the first set of guys to start carrying the crates to the waiting tables and get this started. Any marching orders before we start?" Amanda writes down the instructions to give to the guys.

"Nope, we are good. They know what they are doing. Just keep things moving. It's actually good that this delivery is smaller. Gives us a chance to slowly move up on this process. I heard you tell that driver to be back by six. Do you really think you can get all of that done before then?" Dave asks skeptically.

"That is not a problem for today, but I can't say that will always be the case. Did you also hear that we will get crates every day but Thursday? We need to keep on top of these, or we will get buried. If we don't get crates that are brought in every day done by the end of that day, it will just snowball."

"What will help is if we do find a way the dealers determine which crates the drugs are in by some symbol or stamp of some kind on the crate," Dave says. "That will really help. I doubt the drugs are in every box. Just a choice few. I guess we will see."

"Okay, well, the crates are just about unloaded from the truck, so I need to get this process going. I will talk to you later, Dave." Amanda says to four men standing next to the crates, "Okay, you guys, start lifting these crates onto these tables. You four will be the muscle. You keep watch as they finish a crate have another one waiting and so on. Just keep the flow moving until we are out of crates. The rest of you, start opening crates and be careful not to damage the crates." Amanda checks with the table teams. "So your group opens the crate and pass them on to this group down the table. Kind of assembly-line process. Then you down there at the end, close them up and remove them from the table. You are down there because you four will need to close them back up without damaging them and move them back to this area over there on the floor so they can be picked up again."

Amanda will have this running like a well-oiled clock in a matter of no time. As Dave looks on, he writes notes on things he needs to keep aware of. He is also impressed as to how organized Amanda is with all this. With virtually no planning time, she brought all this together overnight.

Very nice job, he thinks to himself. He must remember to mention this to Greg. *I wonder how they are doing on their part of town.*

"Greg, Dave here. We are all set here. How are things at your end?" Dave says into the phone.

"We are all set and ready for the drugs to arrive. Also, we have the hotel for Carlos just about ready. All the workers are in place. We just need to get some upgrades in a couple of areas to make sure it looks like a hotel instead of an old abandoned wreck. We will have it ready by tonight. Carlos and his crew will be able to move in tomorrow morning. The showdown between the main guy at the museum and Carlos, we figure, will happen at the mock-up hotel, so we need to make it as realistic as possible. When we get to the showdown, we want this place crawling with cops and agents. We want to invite Jimmy and his crew and all of our field agents and have them hidden all over this place so Carlos and his crew are fully protected.

"I know I am jumping the gun a bit, but I want to make sure we have a plan all the way to the end of this. I think once the missing heroin is discovered, things are going to happen quick, so I want everyone on their toes. There will be no room for slipups. Make sure you communicate that to your people on your end. Well, those that will be involved in this sting operation at the hotel—we need to start identifying who those will be from the get-go. I will leave that to you on your end. Carlos and his crew will be in place tomorrow. Make sure everyone that will be at his side for the showdown knows who they are and are ready. Everybody wears a vest. I want no accidents, loss of life, or injuries, except on the drug dealers' side. And not our drug dealer. Will you let everyone know that?" Greg says all out of breath from his soapbox.

"No problem, Greg. I got it. I know who will be involved in that part of the process, and it's none of those opening or closing crates. I will get them ready. Oh, and by the way, George did an awesome job making this building look like the Washington Customs Service warehouse. It looks identical, so if someone from these drug dealers gets suspicious and follow the truck here, they will never think it's anything but business as usual.

"We built this place up so the trucks drive in and are immediately in lockdown. No one can see what they're doing. It's perfect. I thought the trucks leaving the building empty would be an issue, but I have been on the phone with Brett setting this all up exactly the way their operation works, and this is how they do it. The crates are in a holding place for twenty-four hours before they are shipped out. A different truck comes for them and delivers them to the ship or the plane, depending on which way they are going. So we have the operation duplicated exactly the way they do it. We will have these drug dealers going crazy trying to figure out how the drugs were not shipped." Dave is quite satisfied that this plan is going to be epic.

"Okay, perfect. Now next phase will commence in three days. And that will be letting it out that this drug dealer named Carlos has moved into town and has already got a drug operation in the works. They don't need to be rocket scientists to figure out that Carlos has their drugs. We just need to keep their location a real secret for as long as we can. The only ones who know the location of Carlos is Carlos and his crew and you and me. The players at the hotel will not know what they are there for until the eleventh hour. That way, this will be a real secret. No one will know," Greg says with confidence. "Dave, do you see anything I missed or we missed?"

"I am confident we have everything covered. Any idea how long this process will take before they figure it out?" Dave asks.

"We were brainstorming earlier—Trevor and his crew and those of us on this end. And we are thinking this will be a snowball effect and it will be quick. We are thinking once they discover the drugs are missing and that they are missing from all fronts, we think within a week we will have them smoked out. It really depends on just how much drugs we grab and its street value. We want to make sure we take from all of the shipments equally or as equally as we can. A lot will also depend on how many different locations there are. I'm not even going to speculate how many locations there are or where they are. Anything else you need before we go?"

"I think we're good," Dave says as he is inspecting some of the crates while walking by them. "On this end, we have a shipment of thirty crates today, but Brett says they will be probably double tomorrow. It varies from day to day. So we just wait and see what we get each day."

"Okay, Dave. Talk to you later. Let me know if you need anything."

"Sounds good, Greg. Talk to you soon. You do the same," Dave says as he hangs up the phone.

"Eureka!" shouts Logan, one of the many workers challenged to open the crates. "Dave, I think I found what we were looking for. You see this little picture of the key in red ink down here toward the bottom? Well, we have found drugs now in every crate this symbol is on and no drugs in crates that don't have them. We will still open up every crate today, but we can bet then that if we find heroin in every box with this, we should be able to cripple their operation."

"So how much have you folks found in drugs so far?" Dave says to the whole group.

"Well, we have found a lot of big bags of heroin in these boxes," Amanda says. "We did as you instructed and took out what seems like exactly half or a little more if we couldn't make it half. Here's what we have so far." Amanda shows Dave the bins with the bags of heroin in it.

"Is there a way we can calculate the street value of what we have taken? Anyone?" Dave asks the group as a whole.

Another guy pipes up. "I don't know how accurate this is, but I think it's close. If my calculations are correct, we so far have at least two or three hundred thousand dollars in product so far. We did these calculations in class in school last semester as a project, and I was the closest to the right number. And I wasn't too far off the mark. There is a way to figure this out, and I think I have it."

"Okay, we will go with your figures then," Dave says. "What's your name?"

"Mark Reynolds, sir!"

"Okay, Mark Reynolds, thank you. We will leave it to you to do the calculations. So let's put what Mark has calculated aside so we know it is counted and move on. How many more crates do we have to open?"

Amanda pipes up again and says, "We have eight crates left to open and four left to close. We are still going to open all of these crates today, and it will be up to you if you want us to do the same tomorrow. Or are you comfortable with opening only those crates that have this key symbol on the bottom?"

"Well, unless these prove to be not all that accurate—and it appears they are—then I say open only the ones with the key. The only thing that will change that is if we find a crate with a key symbol and no drugs. Then we go back to opening all of them. As long as this holds, let's do it this way. Hopefully, it will hold true and save us from opening more of these crates. Let's get this finished up today though. Its already four o'clock, and we have to have these crates ready for pickup at six o'clock, so let's get moving. Oh, Logan, how many crates so far have you found with the key on it?"

"Of the thirty crates today, only ten had the key on it and the drugs," Logan says. "I have looked at all the crates, and there are no more with the key, so we do not expect to find any more drugs today. But we will keep you informed."

"Thank you, all. You are doing a great job. Keep up the good work. Tomorrow we will expect to see at least double this number of crates. So if that's the case, we should expect to see double the crates with drugs. George, you are logging where these crates are going, right? Just the ones with the drugs of course."

"Sure am, Dave. So far, we only have three locations. That's three locations out of ten crates. Once we are done for the week, I will give you and Greg a list of where they are going. What we are thinking is, they don't go to the same locations every day. We don't even know at this point if drugs are even shipped every day. They may only ship once or twice a week. We won't know until we complete the week. The drugs will not have met their first location from today until Monday next week. That's when the first fallout should happen or shortly after. I would say they will start getting calls from their dealers sometime middle of next week or even sooner. According to these manifests, the first shipment arrives to the Museu Nacional de Belas Artes in Brazil on Monday. Of course, we are not sure how long they are opened after they arrive, but we assume very soon after they arrive," George says while reading the manifest.

"Okay, great. Sounds like we won't be at this more than a couple of weeks. Thanks, George. Let me know if you guys need anything. I have some reports to write so I stay on top of all of this. They want reports right away on this. The top brass is really watching this operation. We can't let anything go wrong. Period!" Dave says.

"Okay, Jason, it's now four p.m. on what, July 13?" Jeanette says to Jason over the phone. "So we have several things we need to get done before the twenty-fifth. Have you spoken to Trevor yet? He is kind of a key component to this wedding, you know. I don't mean to nag, but time is running out. You said he was on this big case right now. You might want to make sure he can get away."

"Yes, ma'am," Jason snorts back. "I will call him right now. Will that satisfy Her Majesty?" Jason says playfully with a big grin on his face.

"Okay, I will let you go so you can do just that. I will talk to you later. Love you, honey."

"Love you too," Jason says as he hangs up the phone.

The phone in Trevor's pocket begins to ring. After he scrambles to answer it, he says, "Hello. This is Trevor."

"Trevor, my old friend, how are you doing today?" Jason says very happily.

"I am doing great, Jason. What are you up to these days?"

"Well, I am calling you to make sure you are available on the evening of July 25," Jason says.

"Let me guess, there is going to be some sort of nuptials going on that day," Trevor says, rather sure of himself.

"That it is. I need a best man, and I won't do this if you are not there with me."

"Well, you know I wouldn't miss this for anything. Of course, I will be there. So where is there, Jason?"

"We are getting married at the Madhatter restaurant," Jason says.

"You're kidding. They are letting you get married in their restaurant, and then what? Have a party?" Trevor asks.

"Well, it's only going to be the two of us, Jeanette, and her sister. For the wedding, it is really small and intimate. As for the party, we are just going to have dinner, the four of us. We really don't have a need for anyone else. There is no one else we are particularly close to. So we thought just a little wedding and then dinner. We intend to invite the wedding officiant to join us for dinner and drinks if he wants. Other than that, just the staff of Madhatter since we have been hanging around there for so long. They know us. So I would imagine they will join in throughout the night. Oh, and they are offering us two meeting rooms as the groom's room and bride's room. That was pretty cool of them."

"One thing, Jason," Trevor says. "I just wanted you to know that I am involved in this big case where I am undercover and I may have to leave early. But I will make sure it's not until after dinner."

"That's fine, Trevor. You do what you have to. I suppose you can't tell me what this big case is you are involved in?" Jason says.

"Sorry, I really am not able to say anything. I can say that this case is somehow connected to Christopher's murder. I just don't know how yet. Other than that, I really can't say. But when it's all over, I will tell you all about it. Right now, there are too many unanswered questions. I really have to go. I will see you on the twenty-fifth. Oh, what time should I be at the Madhatter?"

Jason replies, "Four p.m. would be perfect. The wedding officiant will be there around five o'clock. See you then, Trevor. Be safe, my friend." Jason's voice sounds worried.

As much as Trevor wanted this and hoped for this, Jason also knows what a dangerous job it is that Trevor has now, so he worries about him.

Oh crap, he thinks to himself, *I meant to tell him that the hearing about Sheppard Security is on that following Monday. It just worked out to be right after our wedding.*

Chapter Twenty

Dave walks in on day 3 of the operation where the crates are being searched. In the last two days, they have determined that the only crates that now need to be opened are the ones that have a key at the bottom in red ink. They have seized over what Logan has determined is over a half million dollars in heroin. This is only half of what they found.

It's incredible the amount of heroin going through this place, Dave thinks. *If this is indicative of what they have been shipping through here in the past five years, then oh my god, the amount of poison they have been sending out of here is staggering. What an operation they have going here. We have also determined that there are only four key locations that these drugs have been shipping to. One of them right here in the US to Chicago, probably to cover the domestic trade. This operation is pretty impressive as to how well run it appears to be. Too bad the trade is heroin.*

"Amanda, have all of the drugs confiscated been shipped over to Greg?" Dave asks.

"All except this last batch and that will be heading over there as soon as we open this last crate for today," Amanda says, looking at her clipboard for the numbers. "Here is what we have so far in the past three days. At the rate we are going, we will have over a million dollars in heroin before they realize the first shipment is light. Dave, we are finding that every day we only find drugs in 10 crates. Only 10 each day. Doesn't matter how many crates there are in a day, only 10 have drugs. We are sure of that. Monday we had 30 crates,

Tuesday 68 crates, and today 62 crates. George spoke to Brett, and he said there will be no crates tomorrow, but on Friday, there will be almost 200 crates—196 is what he said we would have. Huge jump but I will bet that with all those crates, there will still only be 10 with heroin. Anyway, we will check every box for the key mark and let you know."

"Okay, thanks, Amanda, and thanks to everyone that has been working hard on this. Keep me posted. I'm going to see how Greg is doing on the other end of town," Dave says.

"Hello. Greg here," Greg says answering the phone on the first ring.

"Greg, Dave. How are things on your end?"

"The hotel is all set up now. We have it so Carlos will be well protected. This old place has a lot of places for us to hide those of us that will be ready for this to come to a head. We chose the perfect spot in the hotel where we can surround the room that Carlos and his crew will be in and not be seen. Now we will just need their top guy to come here and try to kill Carlos. He will want answers and, for sure, his drugs back before he kills him, so we will have that on our side. Plus, no one works in this building without body armor. I want everyone protected. We have a few days though before they start to wonder where their drugs are. They should start getting calls from their dealers by Monday sometime in the afternoon.

"I will reach out to Jimmy from metro. He is going to want to be part of this, and I promised him we would let him be part of the takedown when it came to that. So I will let him in on the action at the hotel when the time comes. Also, the warehouse on this end of town is ready. We are already receiving your shipments of heroin. We are disposing of it. We have no intention of letting them get near any of this, so we should be safe. Where are we at on your end?"

"Well, we are pushing right along," Dave says. "We have had just over 150 crates this week so far, but according to Brett, there won't be any tomorrow but on Friday 196 crates."

He tells Greg about the ten crates and the heroin in them.

"You mean there are only ten crates a day with heroin? Wow, that does surprise me," Greg says. "I would have expected quite a bit more. But it's also kind of smart. If you stick to just that, chances are no one would be the wiser. If you get greedy, that's usually when things go wrong. Okay, well, let me know how things go out there, and I will do the same."

"Sounds good, Greg," Dave says. "Oh, listen. One more thing before I let you go. Actually, two things. First, when are you going to have all of our snitches start spreading the word there is a new drug kingpin in town? And two, are you going to give Jimmy a call and fill him in on what to expect and when?"

"Yes, on Jimmy. I have already filled him in on the game plan. I just need to update him. We are letting the snitches know they need to start spreading the word over the weekend. We need it to be common knowledge by Monday," Greg explains.

"Okay, great. This should be only too obvious to them if they are paying attention at all. Good news. Thanks for the update, Greg." Dave says.

"All right. Talk to you soon. Let me know if anything changes," Greg says.

"Will do," Dave says back. "Talk soon."

"Harvey, it looks like the Feds are going to have this coming to a head real soon," Jimmy says. "Let me fill you in on the plan. I was asked by some of the boys to see if you wanted to be part of this hotel the Feds put together. What do you think? You have your badge, and you are a cop. A very good cop, as I recall. It might give you a chance to nail Rodney if he is really part of all this like you suspect. I was going over your notes and realized that there is too much here to ignore. We are going to be going after him at some point on this. Do you think he has what it takes to be running this whole thing?"

"First, Jimmy, I would love to be part of the Feds party," Harvey says. "Second, I definitely think this Rodney is tied up in this somehow. Do I think he has the smarts to run this whole thing? Not a chance. He might be second-in-command, but there is someone else that we haven't identified yet that is running this whole operation. That's the one we need to nail at the Feds' hotel. That's the one we have to wait for."

"Okay, I agree and am glad to have you there with us," Jimmy says. "Greg from the FBI is going to be calling me tonight to fill me in on where we are at. Trevor is going to be playing the role of the drug dealer. Apparently, this whole plan was his idea. The Feds are letting him be the one in the spotlight. So he is now Carlos Ross. They will not be putting him in the hotel until we are ready for this to end. In the meantime, he will be helping with the heroin on Greg's side of town. They have quite an operation going. Apparently, they have seized over a half million dollars' worth of heroin so far."

Jimmy answers the phone. "This is Jimmy."

"Jimmy, this is Greg. Wanted to give you an update on where we are at. We are continuing to remove heroin from crates earmarked for these four locations," Greg says to Jimmy in the phone. "But we are only finding a maximum of ten crates per day regardless of how many total crates there are. There will not be any crates tomorrow. For some reason, they don't ship crates on Thursday. Don't know why but okay. This weekend, we are having the snitches that you provided, as well as our own, start spreading the word about Carlos. So by Monday, it should be common knowledge.

"I will keep you notified as to where we are. But be ready to move as soon as this starts to come to a head. We will need everyone at the hotel and ready for anything. One thing, everyone that is part of this party must wear body armor. No exceptions. We do not know what to expect, so we need to be ready for whatever. Agreed?"

"Definitely agreed. I am getting my best people on this. So when you are ready, give us the word and as much lead time as you can. How's this hotel of yours?" Jimmy asks.

"It's good. There is this place in the hotel that we have picked out for Carlos that will have hiding places all around him so we can keep hidden from whomever until we don't need to be anymore."

"Okay, great. Just let me know and we will be there. And thanks, Greg. I know you are under no obligation to include us. I appreciate that you are."

"Don't thank me," Greg responds back. "Thank Trevor. He said you would be a great addition to this team, and you have been part of it, so he wanted to include you. I couldn't have agreed more. So welcome to the team. Bring as many cops along as you can spare."

"Sounds good, Greg. Thanks again. We won't let you down. Talk to you soon." Jimmy hangs up the phone.

"Greg, I wanted to let you know about a commitment I have next Saturday. My best friend is getting married, and I am his best man," Trevor tells Greg. "It will only be on that afternoon. Four p.m. to whenever. I should be available to leave if I need to anytime after six p.m., I would think. I know Jason would understand."

"Nonsense," Greg says. "You stay and have a great time. I don't see a need to have you there anytime earlier. What's nice about this setup is that we can decide when you need to make an entrance. I am saying only his underlings will be scoping things out on the kingpin's behalf and reporting back to him. We can determine when you need to be there. So no worries."

"Great. Thanks," Trevor says. "That will make my friend Jason very happy. Okay, I am out of here for now unless you need me for anything."

"Nope, go enjoy your evening. We are shutting down here in a few anyway. We just got the last of the heroin for the night. We are going to get this cataloged and take off ourselves. So good night," Greg says to a departing Trevor.

"Amanda, why don't you call it a night?" Dave says. "We got the rest of this. We are going to shut things down anyway for tonight and reopen for business on Friday morning. Everyone needs to be back here on Friday morning at seven a.m., no later. First shipment of the day is at eight. And then we will be seeing shipments almost every hour on the hour all day. Remember, 196 crates on Friday. I wouldn't expect our 10—if that's all we see of the heroin crates—all in one load. They will be spread out throughout the day, I'm sure. So go home, everyone. See you on Friday." Dave finishes up what he was doing on the tables and gets things finalized for the day.

Chapter Twenty-One

"Jason, are you ready for Saturday?" Trevor says. "It's Monday and less than a week from your wedding day."

Trevor puts the phone down on speaker as he gets ready to go to work. *Today could be a big day,* he thinks to himself. *Today, Greg says these drug dealers will start to get the word from their shipments that half of their expected heroin is missing. This should be a really bad day for these drug dealers.*

"I wanted to let you know that I haven't forgotten about you and that you are on my mind as someone getting married end of the week," Trevor says. "I also wanted you to know that I went out and got my tux rented on Saturday. It should be ready by Thursday. You know, Jason, one question." Trevor asks a not-all-that-serious question, "If it's only the four of us, why did we need to rent a tuxedo? It just seems silly for only four people at the wedding."

"It's what Jeanette wanted. She thought it would be nice if we all got dressed up for this. I think it's a great idea. Don't be raining on her parade, Trevor," Jason says with a playful sound in his voice.

"I'm not, I'm not. Hey, I went out and rented one, didn't I? I was just asking."

"Okay then. Anything else going on, Trevor?"

"I wanted you to know that because of this big case I am on right now, I may have to leave early on Saturday even though my boss says no," Trevor says.

"What is this case you're involved in anyway?" Jason asks.

"Well, what I can say is that this is all going to tie into the death of Christopher. There is a lot more going on at the historical museum than just the murder of my friend. There is a lot of drug activity going on over there. A lot!"

"Wow, really? So you are going to be part of a huge drug sting, huh?"

"Something like that. Say, when is that hearing on the status of your security agency?" Trevor asks.

"That's the crazy thing, it's on the Monday after my wedding, like next Monday. It's at ten a.m. You will be able to be there, right? You are my main witness. Without you, there is no chance the judge will rule in my favor. They need expert testimony as to what went down. Coming from me, they would only see that as self-serving."

"Don't worry. I will be there. But I think I will be out of touch for a while after that though. Greg, my boss, thinks this whole case is going to come to a head very soon, and when it does, it's going to be epic. Just as long as it's a success for our side," Trevor says.

"Harvey, have you been listening to the scuttlebutt around this department? The activity over the weekend was pretty intense according to one of my snitches," Jimmy says with a lot more force than he intended. "He was actually afraid for his life. He said the local drug talent has been getting pretty nasty over the last couple of days. There is word on the street that a lot of heroin is missing, and there are huge drug enforcers getting really mean to a lot of what we would call street people. The drifters and drug users."

"Jimmy, we've been hearing about it all morning that there's a new drug king in town. That's what they are calling him. Well, Greg's plan worked. It's all over town," Harvey says with a sign of satisfaction.

"I need to call Greg and see what they are hearing. This is great news," Jimmy says. "I'm really curious to see how this all changes when they find out they are missing over a million dollars' worth of their product."

"This is Greg," Greg says as he grabs the phone.

"Greg, it's Jimmy. We are getting a lot of talk out here about the new drug king that's in town. That's what our snitches are calling him. New drug king. That seems to have latched on. Trevor is a hit. And not in a good way either. What have you heard on your end?"

"Pretty much the same thing," Greg says. "Everybody is talking about it. Boy, they did a great job getting it out this weekend. It really did become the talk of town. I can see this becoming a huge problem to the current drug kingpin. Well, we got what we wanted. Now let's hope we get the results we are looking for once they start hearing their heroin is a little short. They are going to want fast action as to what happened to it. Did I tell you what we have taken so far? As of today, we have seized over one million dollars' worth of heroin. That's what our man on Dave's team is calculating it at. He has some education on how to calculate these kinds of measurements. So we are pretty sure it's fairly accurate. They are going to be hopping mad when they hear from their distributors that they are missing so much product. Of course, they won't know about all of it at once. They will learn today they are missing only about $150,000 by today. They will learn about the rest as the week moves on. We will be taking heroin every day this week for sure. So they will be down, oh, I would say, million and a half of product by week's end or more. I will keep you updated as we push on."

"I will let you know if anything happens on our front if you could do the same," Jimmy says. "I have a feeling once this becomes a real crisis for these drug dealers, the shit's going to hit the fan fast. We will need to be ready. All of us."

"Agreed, Jimmy," Greg says. "Thanks. I will talk to you soon."

"Dave here," Dave says in the phone as he picks it up.

"Dave, Greg. Well, the street network is all a bustle today. Everybody apparently is talking about this new drug king that has moved into town and taken over a big part of the DC business. I just heard from Jimmy at metro. He was saying the same thing. And these drug dealers have not even heard they are missing product yet. That should be in the next couple of hours. When they do, the shit will really hit the fan and in a big way. Jimmy was saying that the way these street people are talking, these drug dealers will go ballistic once they learn about their missing product. He thinks this is going to hit the streets really fast and hard. We need to be ready for it. He thinks it's going to be faster than we think. He just thinks we need to be really careful and prepared for this to go down a lot sooner than later."

"I agree with Jimmy. I think we may have underestimated how soon this is going to hit the streets," Dave says with some concern. "These drug dealers are going to hit the streets fast and hard. They are going to be in crisis mode when they find out how much of their product is missing."

"I have briefed Trevor on this, and he has been here working on the drugs process as it comes in from your team. I think we might want to get him out of here. Look, it's Monday. We know what's going to happen later today. We should just make sure he is inaccessible. Even though they don't know who he is, I think we need him out of here just the same. What are your thoughts on that?" Greg asks.

"Yeah, I agree. Send him home. That's his safest place right now. No one knows him outside of this world."

"Okay, will do. With any luck, he will put in an appearance end of the week, and this will be all over by the weekend."

"According to the manifests, the last shipment from last week will arrive at its locations by Wednesday," Dave says. "Thursday at the latest. By then, they will be all over the place trying to figure out how their drug shipments were compromised."

"One more thing before I let you go. How secure is that building you are in as far as once the truck gets into the dock area? Are you in total lockdown? I am thinking these dealers are not stupid. They will try to follow the trucks that pick up the crates at the museum."

"Don't worry," Dave says. "There is no way they will get in here. It's impregnable. The trucks go in and virtually disappear within these walls. There is no way for them to get in here. The trucks come in through an underground driveway from several blocks away. They will never find us. This place was built during the old Prohibition days. There are tunnels all over this part of the city. We can't be touched here. That's why I chose here. We have used this place before to bring in very high-profile witnesses and very high-profile drug leaders that are going on trial. This place is great."

"Sounds like that is the perfect place for what we are doing," Greg says. "Okay, so we appear to be perfectly secure on that side of town. We can rely on word of mouth how to find Carlos. We will leak that little by little. Our snitches are telling us that they will help us in maintaining the information as we give it out, so they will only release information as we give it. For now, we have only released the fact that there is a new drug king in town and that he is hitting the heroin market with a big bang. So we just need to release the next bit of information in about three days, maybe two. A lot depends on how much the snitches hear in the next day or so. If they are getting a lot of activity or getting pressured, we may have to provide them with updated information sooner."

"Well, just make sure that we don't reveal where to find Carlos until the very last bit of information. We want that final showdown to be when we decide. You know, Greg, I would feel a whole lot better if we knew how that was. We suspect this Rodney as being high up in that chain, but we really don't know who beyond that," Dave says with some frustration.

"I know, Dave. I wish we had better intel too, but according to our snitches on the street, they don't know any more than we do. They can probably put us onto a couple of the more local guys that are doing some of the dirty work for this kingpin, but that's pretty much it. That might change as this whole situation heats up. I told them that we don't feel that need right now but maybe later. I guess at this point, it's a wait-and-see game."

"That's how I see it as well. Okay, well, I will let you go for now. We are sending over some more shipments of heroin for you. We are over the million-dollar mark now. Way over. I have one of my guys who seems pretty good at this. An agent named Logan has been calculating these drugs for us. It's staggering how much is going through there. Thanks, Greg. Talk to you later."

"You too, Dave. Let me know if anything changes," Greg says in reply.

Jeanette is spending the day with her sister, getting things ready for her wedding. The dress has been ordered and will be ready tomorrow. This is her final fitting. The dressmaker assures her she will have the dress in time.

"Bernadette, what do you think? Will Jason be okay with knowing what I used to do for a living?" Jeanette says as she slips the dress over her head. "You and Trevor are the only ones that know right now, but Trevor is going to tell Jason on Saturday. I am so worried that when he tells him, Jason might go ballistic and not want to marry me. I don't like that Trevor has waited so long to tell him, but he has been out of town for training and now he is on a huge case that is going to keep him busy right up to the time of the wedding. He promised he will tell him before we get married on Saturday. I am really worried."

"If he really loves you, and I really believe he does, I don't think it will matter. He might go nuts on Saturday before the wedding, but I don't see him calling this whole wedding off because of it. When did you stop doing that as a living?" Bernadette says with a little discretion in her voice.

Jeanette laughs a little and says, "You can say it, little sister. When did I stop hooking for a living?" She laughs some more and says, "I haven't been hooking now for three or four months. And then I was only doing just certain high-priced customers. But I eventually weaned off of them too. So I am currently living on my savings, but I am looking for something permanent. Any ideas?"

"Actually, I do have an idea. I remember you telling me all that happened to Jason with his former partner and his sister. What if you were to go work for Jason if that fits for Jason. Of course, a lot is going to depend on how he reacts on Saturday when Trevor tells him about your occupation. But if he still wants to marry you and I am going to bet that after he is done being all pissed off about it, he will still want to marry you. After all, everybody has a past. Everybody has had boyfriends in the past. You just have had a few hundred more than most," Bernadette says, trying to lighten the mood a little.

"Yeah, you're right, but I have a feeling he is not going to look at it like that. Big difference from having a lot of boyfriends and being a hooker and fucking everyone for money. I really don't see him taking this really easy. I just hope after Trevor tells him, he will give me the chance to explain and talk to him about it. That's why I insisted on having Jason and Trevor there earlier than needed so Trevor can explain and then so can I. Fingers crossed."

"You know, big sister, you could have avoided this by just telling Jason yourself. I mean, really, Jeanette, why put all this on Trevor? You big chicken. Now you are at the wedding, and when Trevor tells Jason, what if he reacts badly and storms out of there? You give him no chance to get used to the idea, and it may just end up ruining your whole day. Was not telling him worth that?" Bernadette says with quite a bit of force.

She has a point, Jeanette thinks.

If she had told him herself, then whatever happens on Saturday may be avoided, assuming the day ends badly as Bernadette says.

Well, I can't tell him now, Jeanette thinks. *What would be my excuse? Or am I just making more excuses for myself? I know. I will mention it to Trevor and see what he thinks. Maybe Trevor can tell him before Saturday. No, that won't work. This is definitely something he will want to say in person, and he probably won't get the chance to see him in person until Saturday. Boy, I screwed this up big time, and now I am so scared of how he will react. Well, nothing I can do about it at this late stage. It's already Wednesday, and in three days, we get married. He is busily trying to get his shit together for the hearing on Monday. Trevor is out on this big case doing who knows what right now.*

"Okay, well, I have been thinking, and yes, you are right. I really fucked up on this one. I should have had the guts to tell him myself instead of having Trevor do it. Well, it's way too late now. It's already Wednesday, and we get married in three days."

"Dave, we have been fielding snitches for two days now. They are hearing all sorts of mad action stuff going on, and some of them are scared," Greg says with a note of concern in his voice. "These dealers are pissed they are missing so much dope. Quite frankly, Jimmy has had to put some of them in protective custody because they are so afraid of the streets right now. These dealers are hopping mad and want the heads of whoever took their drugs. The problem for them is, they don't know yet who did take them, and no one is telling them anything. So they are getting madder by the hour."

"Can we hold this off for another couple days, or are we saying we need to act on this sooner than later?" Dave says back in the phone.

"I would like to try to hold this off at least one more day if we can. We knew it was going to happen like this. So we need to stick to our guns. If we have to provide police protection to some of these street snitches, then we do it. We intentionally did not tell the street snitches more than they needed to know so they can't blow this for us. I say, tomorrow or Friday, we release the last bit of knowledge to our snitches, like where to find the dealer taking all the dope. Carlos. We will reveal that as soon as we are ready. I mean we have everything and everyone ready and in place in the hotel ready for the showdown that is certain to happen. I think we can hold off one or two more days with them getting even more mad. The great news is, they don't know who to get mad at. No one on the street knows. They can torture these people, but they can't reveal what they don't know," Greg says with all certainty.

"Okay, I am with you on this, Greg. I think we hold out. I would talk to Jimmy though and let him know in case he doesn't hear all that is going on right now, but I think he probably has his ear to the streets more than we do. You want to give him a call, Greg?"

"Yeah, I will take care of that, Dave. I will also brief Trevor and his crew to be ready. He has a wedding he is standing up for his best friend on Saturday, so I am sure he would appreciate us ending this before then or not putting this showdown right in the middle of this wedding. I think he needs to be at the wedding by five o'clock on Saturday."

"Since we can control when all this happens, that shouldn't be a problem. Let's plan on this all coming to a head Friday afternoon," Dave says.

"Dave, I think I am going to come to you so we can put a closer strategy together for this. I think we can stop what we are doing. We made the impact we were hoping for. So get a hold of Brett and tell him that he can resume business as usual. Close up your side of this slowly. Don't do it abruptly because we don't know if that building is being watched or not. In fact, I think we can stay with what we are doing until after this all comes to a head. We will wait until after this is all wrapped up to close everything down. I just don't want to take any chances this late in the game. Unless you think we should go a different route."

"Nope, I am with you. No sense in rocking the boat now. We are only talking a couple of days," Dave says in agreement.

"Okay, then I will see you here. When, Greg?"

"I will be there first thing in the morning," Greg says. "I take it you will be leaving shortly, plus with rush hour now, it will be over an hour before I can get there. So I will see you in the morning. In fact, meet me at my office around eight."

"Sounds good. Have a good night," Dave says.

"Okay, Trevor, I don't know how much you heard, but we are coming to a head on this very soon. Probably tomorrow or Friday. More than likely Friday though. In the afternoon. We will have you up there ready with your crew. Meet Dave and I at the office in the morning at eight. We will go over the plan. I am also going to have Jimmy and his crew meet us there also. I want everyone on this showdown party at the office so everyone knows what we are doing and so there are no mistakes. With the stakes this high, we do not want any mistakes, none. In an operation like this, mistake means people die. I will not have that on my watch. We will make sure everyone and every part of this is well defined so everyone knows exactly what they are doing. Have a good night, and see you in the morning. We are shutting this operation down as of tonight. We are leaving Dave's operation up and running until this is over. We can't be sure anyone is watching that building. So nothing changes over there until this is over."

"Hello, this is Jimmy."

"Jimmy, this is Greg. How are you doing today?"

"I'm good, Greg. Was your plan successful? Did you get them going crazy looking for who took their heroin?"

"Oh yeah. Better than we thought. Dave was saying that your snitches were getting pretty good intel," Greg says. "How many of these street snitches have you had to put into police protection?"

"Not all that many," Jimmy says. "Only a couple of ladies that were afraid because the person threatening them was actually threatening their children. We can't have that. The women are snitches as a payback for leniency, but their children shouldn't have to pay for that, so we are protecting them. They are off the street for now. And then there was a couple of our older snitches who were a little afraid but not all that much. We just wanted to get them off the street for now. Other than that, not so much. So what's up with you today?"

"Well, I am calling to let you know we are having a big meeting at our offices in the federal building tomorrow morning at eight. Anyone that is going to be a part of the big finale needs to be at our offices at that time. We are going to have a big strategy meeting because we are bringing this to a head for the final showdown Friday afternoon. We want to make sure everyone that will be there is aware of everything going down and are clear on everything we are doing and what's at stake. I want no mistakes on this. Everyone needs to know. If they can't be there tomorrow, they can't be part of the finale. Period. We can't bend on that. I don't want any mistakes. Mistakes means people get hurt and maybe dead. Not on my watch. That's why we have to be this definitive on this. No meeting, no finale. So, Jimmy, how many of your guys are going to be part of this? I know you and your man Harvey are for sure, but I need a head count so we can plan for this right."

"I understand. I have seven confirmed besides Harvey and I. So nine in all. And we will all be there in the morning. In fact, I will bring the rolls. Courtesy of the metro police. Hey, we know you don't have to include us. We appreciate that you are. I am thinking this will also close the investigation of Christopher's murder as well," Jimmy says.

"More than likely. For now, let's concentrate on this setup and get these drug dealers," Greg says.

"Okay, we will see you in the morning, Greg. Thanks. Good night," Jimmy says as he hangs up.

Chapter Twenty-Two

"Good morning, everyone. I want to welcome the DEA agents here, Jimmy, and the Metropolitan Police Department. You can all get acquainted later. Oh, and by the way, not that its some sort of thing with the police but Jimmy brought the donuts and rolls and we got the coffee. So thank you, Jimmy. For those of you that are along for the ride, let me introduce myself and the local director of the Drug Enforcement Administration, better known as the DEA. I am Greg Stanton, and this is David Stewart. This is a joint combined operation. Let me lay it out for you in a nutshell, and then I will tell you what we have in mind.

"We have this drug dealer who has been using the historical museum as his own personal drugstore. He has been shipping heroin out through international channels for—we figure—five years or more. About two weeks ago, Dave and his team and me and my team set up a sting operation to seize half of the drugs he has been shipping. Throughout these past two weeks, we have seized more than a million and a half dollars' worth of heroin from those shipments. We contacted the courier who picks up the customs orders from the museum and delivers them to the shipyards or the airport, depending on which mode of travel the crates are going. We set up an operation to have the courier drop the crates off with us first, we opened the crates and what drugs we found, and we seized exactly half of their shipments. That operation took two weeks about, and in those two weeks, you see what we seized and that was only half. The amount of heroin they have been smuggling out of DC in the past five years is staggering. That comes to a close tomorrow.

"Fast-forward to today. We have a hotel in Dupont Circle that was an old, abandoned building, which we use as a safe house from time to time. This building is one step away from being condemned. We own it because this is a great place to hide witnesses. We have turned this building into a hotel for our new drug dealer that has come to town and taken all these drugs from these dealers. Everyone, meet our drug dealer, Carlos. Carlos is actually Trevor, a new agent of ours in the FBI with a very impressive training record. Graduated top of his class. We are very proud of him, and before anyone says anything about us putting a rookie in this kind of an undercover position, this whole idea was his. So we are letting him be the bad guy for his first assignment. So, everyone, this is Trevor Andrews."

Greg pauses for everyone to greet him and wish him well.

"Okay," Greg continues, "so we have put the word on the street that there is a new dealer that has been dealing in a large quantity of heroin, and that is just after he arrived here. Without saying so, we had our snitches imply that the missing drugs are the drugs this new dealer has been selling. It has been a very well-orchestrated plan to make sure the right dealers know that Carlos has their drugs. We have been very careful to not reveal where he can be found. That is until tomorrow. Tomorrow around ten or so, Jimmy is going to let it out to all the snitches the location of this drug dealer, Carlos. Before then, we are going to set up the hotel with all of you. The part of the hotel we have designated for Carlos and his crew to be in will have a whole variety of places for all of us to hide. We will all be staking this place out to ensure that no one gets hurt or dead. So here is the plan as to where everyone will be at within this area of the hotel. Now look at this diagram."

Greg shows everyone the diagram of the hotel room and area surrounding this room with all the hidden spots within it.

"Okay, so we need everyone at the hotel by ten a.m.," Dave says. He has taken over this part of the operation. "The reason for this is we are not leaking Carlos's location until then. We believe this is going to happen really fast. These dealers are going out of their mind trying to figure out who has their drugs and where he is. We don't want agents going in there after we leak it out because we believe this is going to go down really fast. Now here is the plan. Several of you are going to be in this lobby area. We need to identify who will be doing this part. Before you volunteer, this is what we have in mind. Does anyone have any doubt they will identify the leader or, as they call him, the kingpin of this operation?"

Pretty much everyone raises their hands.

Greg says, "It's a forgone conclusion. Everyone can pretty much figure out right away who the leader is. The one giving the orders."

"Exactly," Dave continues. "I need eight guys in the lobby that don't look like Feds, and when their underlings come in, take them out quietly and out a back way. We have that all marked for you. Do I have volunteers for this assignment?"

Several agents and cops raise their hands.

"Okay, you, you, you three and you three," Dave says as he points out those eight volunteers, "you will want to dress like you are homeless and just hanging around the lobby because you have no place else to go. Make sure—and this goes for everyone in this room—you are all wearing your body armor. I want no one going in there unprotected. I want no accidents and no fatalities. I want this operation to be a complete success. And we can do this. Okay, so to continue, those of you in the lobby be hanging in a way where you look like you're just hanging, but when these underlings of his—I'm going to call our king pin Mr. X—come in the building, grab them and keep them quiet. When we get there in the morning, I will show everyone where to be. For you eight, I will show you where to bring these enforcers of Mr. X. There is a room we are going to take them to get them handcuffed and gagged so they can't make any noise. Greg?"

"Thanks, Dave. Before I move on to the next section, any questions on this part?"

"I have one question," Logan says. "We take them to this room in the back. How long do we need to hold them there? I assume we are taking them to the police station or FBI holding."

"Very good question, Logan. Yes, they will actually be going to the metro police station. We are giving all the underlings to Jimmy and his crew. A bonus for them for helping us with all this. Mr. X and his top guys will be going to FBI headquarters here in Washington, DC, to the holding cells where all federal prisoners are held in custody. Thanks for bringing that up, Logan. Okay, so once you eight have the underlings out of there, we are hoping that Mr. X and his heavies will come in wondering where their guys are. We will let them go upstairs. Now we don't know if the head guys are going to come in or not. So we need a second level of defense. Here's what we have in mind." Greg shows the second map on the wall to the men, pointing to a diagram of a hallway and a set of rooms. "Carlos will be on the fourth floor. Now there is a reason we have him on the fourth floor. We want to be able to determine who is coming up before they get to Carlos. So on the second floor, we will have men hiding in this room and this room and over here." Greg points out different areas of the map. "Okay, you will be on silent coms to make sure no one can hear you as they pass you by. You are basically lookouts. You need to alert everyone on the next floors whether they need to grab those coming up or let them through.

"Now, guys, this is really important. You have to decide if those coming up include Mr. X or not. If not, then you need to alert those on the next floor to grab them as quietly as they did on the first floor. Now is there anyone that feels they would be able to, without a doubt, determine if it's Mr. X or not? We need to make a positive ID."

"Greg, listen, I have a better idea. I have a snitch that can positively ID Mr. X. Why don't I get ahold of him tonight and bring him in and show us a picture of him? I can talk to him after this meeting today," Jimmy says.

"Excellent. And you are sure he has seen him and can positively ID him? You are absolutely certain?" Greg asks.

"Yes, and I know where he is during the day. I will get a picture of him so we can get it to the person making the ID. Will that make it easier for everyone?" Jimmy says to the room.

"Jimmy, get that to me. I will make the ID," Harvey says.

"Okay, Harvey, it's all yours," Jimmy says. "In fact, I will tell you who the snitch is and where to find him. You can go get what you need from him yourself. Fair enough?"

"Deal!" Harvey exclaims. "So show me on this map where you want me to be to make the ID. I want a place where I can clearly see him but he cannot see me."

Greg points to the place on the map where he will be able to see the best.

"Okay, so that takes care of identifying Mr. X," Greg says. "Anyone with Mr. X will be allowed to go through to the fourth floor. Anyone else will be stopped on the third floor just like those on the first floor. Just remember, to all of you grabbing these underlings, keep them quiet. If you have to knock them out, then do it but do it quietly. The reason there are so many of you is, I want more than one on each. That will ensure success and keep them under our control. We don't expect there to be too many henchmen going in first. We should be fine. Now to be sure we are fine, there will be those working or at least appearing to be working the hotel, like the clerk behind the desk, the person behind the cage handing out the keys to residents or guests, and so on so there will be extras in the lobby if you need them. Okay, any questions on those instructions?

"Okay, good. Now we need about the same number of you on the third floor and for the lookouts, I want to see one at the beginning of the hallway right past the stairs. Harvey, you have your place, and it's right where the hallway turns to go upstairs. I also want a backup on the second floor just in case. Make sure you all keep quiet and out of sight. On the third floor, I want the same number of you—eight in various parts of this floor. There are rooms that are intentionally busted up so that they can't be rented out, so we have plenty of places for you to hide. We will help you get placed when we all get there.

"Okay, now for the fourth floor. This will be Carlos's floor. He will be at the end of the hallway, the farthest distance from the stairs. That, of course, is also by design. We want him farther away from the stairs so we can size it up. Now Carlos will be in the room with his crew, his henchmen. We have seven separate places to hide within that room alone. It will be made to look like an office for him, but there are rooms inside of the room including a bathroom. The bathroom in this room does work and will have agents waiting inside. Carlos will be at a rackety old desk, and his henchmen will be playing cards at a table in front and to the side of Carlos, making him visible to the door but not a direct line of sight. We don't want Mr. X to come in shooting. If he doesn't have a clear line of fire, he won't start shooting. Plus, he is going to want to know where his drugs are first. Now once they come past the second floor, Harvey, you will need to let Dave and myself know via the silent com. The table where they are playing cards will be in front, but his henchmen will be standing in front of Carlos and just to his left and right with their guns drawn but in a downward position. So basically, nonconfrontational but ready. Dave and about ten men plus myself will all be in that room but out of sight, guns drawn and ready. That's all I can give you at this point. We really don't know what to expect once Mr. X. gets in that room, but we want to be ready for anything."

Greg has brilliantly laid out the plan with the help of Dave and showed their men what the entire plan is and where everyone will be during this operation. Greg is satisfied that everyone knows their roles.

"Does anyone have any questions or comments on this operation? Or does anyone have a problem with this plan?"

Several of them raised their hands.

"Sirs, I think I speak for everyone here," Harvey says. "We think this plan is brilliant and will be very successful, and we will get this scum off the streets and be rid of this poison. Thank you for bringing all of us into this. We know that you didn't have to bring metro into this, and we appreciate that you did. We are proud to be a part of this."

"Harvey, it is our pleasure. I am looking forward to this being over and a huge success. One final thought before I call it for today. A reminder, everyone must wear their body armor tomorrow. That is nonnegotiable. And don't forget I want everyone in the hotel and in place by ten a.m. Jimmy, leave the snitches to someone that is not part of this operation to get the word on the streets. Make sure there is no doubt that they will find out quickly where to find Carlos. Harvey, get that ID of Mr. X today and don't worry about showing any of us what he looks like. As long as you can ID him, that's all we need. We will know who he is once he passes the third floor. If there's nothing further, I will leave it there and bid us all a very good day tomorrow. Good night everyone," Greg says.

Greg and Dave get a lot of slapping on the back and handshakes as the agents and cops exit the room. Carlos also gets a lot of handshakes as they pass by him. Jimmy goes back to the precinct with Harvey, and they get the information Harvey needs to identify Mr. X. Jimmy puts in motion the information for the snitches and the group of cops that will be doling out the word to these street people. *Snitch* is actually a word that they use for anyone that helps the police to either get out of some trouble or are just those individuals that enjoy helping the cops out and know the right people to make it worth the cops' while. Mostly though, they are people that have gotten in trouble of one kind or another, and this is the bargain they made with the cops for a lighter sentence or community service to keep them out of jail. They cooperate because there is always the threat of going to jail if they don't.

"Jeanette, did you want me to go with you to pick up your wedding dress?" Bernadette says on the phone.

"Yeah, that would be great, Bernadette. I would love that."

"Did you want to meet me at my house?" Jeanette says.

"Yep, on my way. I will be there in about an hour or so. Then we can go and make sure everything fits this Friday morning. One final fitting and you are getting married, big sister. Yes!"

"I know. Hard to believe. Never thought that would ever happen to me. Plus, it made me completely change my lifestyle. Now let's hope Jason doesn't kick me to the curb. Does he really need to know, Bernadette? I mean I quit that business. What if we just didn't tell him? Would that be an option?" Jeanette asks.

"Well, let me ask you this then, Jeanette," Bernadette says. "Do you really want to start out your married life with that huge lie as your foundation for your new married life? I mean, you have to ask yourself, 'Do I really want to hide this from Jason?' Also, think about this. What happens if this comes out a year or two or whatever after you are married? How will you explain that to Jason in, like, two years? These are things you should be thinking about before you decide to keep this from him now. Just saying, Jeanette, you probably don't want to start out with this humungous lie as the undertone for your entire marriage. You should do what you think is best. That's all I am saying. Think about your decision and decide if this is something you are prepared to live with. If you want my two cents, I say let Trevor tell Jason and let the chips fall where they may. He loves you, and you love him. Trust him. Okay, I am going to stop talking now. You do what you want. I am retiring my soapbox. Besides, I am pulling into your driveway. Why don't you come out and we can go? I'll drive." Bernadette hangs up.

"Good morning, everyone!" Greg says as agents and police alike start filing into the old hotel. "Dave is upstairs and will show you where to go and what you will be watching."

As the eight agents and officers come into the lobby area, Greg shows them where they need to be. At the same time, he is sending other agents and officers upstairs for Dave to position. Trevor is already upstairs with Brandon, Steve, and Austin—his crew.

"Harvey, you better get over to the hotel," Jimmy says. "Let Greg and Dave know that I will be there as soon as I wrap up the snitch network here. I am getting the last bit of information out to our snitches. At this point, that includes snitches from Greg and Dave, as well as ours. I will be along shortly. Make sure we have everyone before you go. I don't want to miss anyone. We want this to be well covered. I will see you in a few."

"Sounds good, Jimmy. I will let Greg and Dave know," Harvey says as he is walking out the door. "You are going to be in the room with Trevor and his crew, so you need to be there before anyone gets there, at least the bad guys."

"I know. I will be out the door in five minutes," Jimmy says back to a departing Harvey.

"Dave," Greg says in the walkie-talkie. "You all set up there? Do we have anyone missing up there, or do we need anyone else up there? I have some extras down here."

"I have everyone we expected, but if you have extras, send them my way. I can place them. Never hurts to have extra muscle. Is everyone in place down there? Including the hotel clerk and the other extras in the lobby?"

"Yeah, everyone is here," Greg says in the walkie. "We are well covered down here. This lobby looks like a homeless shelter. We are well covered with hoboes, drunks, and the homeless. When these guys come in, they won't have a chance."

"Okay, once Jimmy gets here, we will be all set," Dave says. "Trevor and the boys are already up there and ready. Plus, everyone hiding in their room is in place with Jimmy as the only exception. Harvey just got here and told me he was five minutes behind him. He was wrapping up what he calls the snitch network. Once that's covered, he will be along. He is giving final instructions. By the way, everyone looks great. They look the part. They obviously know what they are doing because they all came dressed for the part. Very impressive."

"Great, same thing down here. They all look exactly the way they are supposed to. Amazing bunch of cops," Greg responds back in the walkie-talkie.

"Okay, Dave, here comes Jimmy. He is on his way up. Make sure you get him in the right place. Now it's just a waiting game. I am on my way up. I will be in the hiding spots with Jimmy, and so are you. I will pick you up on the way. Harvey has that level covered."

"Okay, we need to turn these off now," Dave says.

"We want no chance of these going off," Greg replies one last time.

"Right. Turning mine off now. See you upstairs in a minute."

Greg climbs the stairs to meet up with Jimmy, Dave, Trevor, and his boys on the fourth floor.

"Greg, Dave, and Jimmy, can you hear me? This is Harvey. I am on the soft com. Wanted to make sure you can hear me clearly at this volume," Harvey says into the mike.

"I can hear you, and I am getting the thumbs-up from the others too," says Jimmy.

"Perfect. I think we are ready. I have a perfect picture of the head guy, so I will know when he walks in," Harvey responds back.

Greg thinks to himself, *We could be waiting here all day. The snitch network, as Jimmy calls, it has had the information now for over an hour. It's only a matter of time now. This is the part I hate. Waiting. Well, this is part of law enforcement.*

"Okay, everyone, heads up. There's activity outside," Logan says into his soft com from the lobby. "There are four men coming in."

As soon as these men come in, Logan and several other agents and cops grab them at gunpoint with their guns at their throats.

"Don't make a sound. Not a peep or you will die right here," an agent downstairs tells the men entering.

They grab them and escort them out the back, putting them into a room and gagging them and handcuffing them to radiators that are built into the floor. It took all 8 agents to get them out of here. In the meantime, those in the lobby are still watching for anyone else. For right now, it's clear. Doesn't mean there aren't more outside. As they secure the four men in the back, Logan stays in the room with them and makes sure they are quiet. The others run back out to the lobby to handle everyone else. As soon as they get back to the lobby, two more men come in guns drawn but in a downward position. The guns may be nonthreatening, but they were out. Four agents grab them and take them back to the same room the same way as the other four men, gagged and kept quiet. Everyone is handcuffed and secured.

Logan watches everyone. They all run back out to the lobby. Still no one else comes in. So they are keeping to their undercover look in the lobby. Logan says into his soft com that they now have six men being held. None of them look smart enough to be in charge of all this. Harvey did share with the lobby agents who they are looking for, so everyone in the lobby knows exactly who they are looking for. They will keep grabbing guys until the right one shows up.

Max, another of the agents in the lobby, reaches into his shirt to say softly, "Heads up, everyone. Our kingpin just came through the door. We are ignoring him and letting him go. Harvey, he's coming your way with three of his henchmen. He is definitely the one on the photo you showed us this morning."

Harvey watches for him and identifies him right away and lets Jimmy, Dave, and Greg know. Greg has moved Trevor out of the room so he is not right there for the taking. Brandon, Steve, and Austin will take it from here. Steve takes his seat at the desk with Brandon and Austin on either side of him. Steve leans back on his chair as Mr. X walks through the door.

He looks down at Steve. "I want my drugs back, and I will kill everyone that gets in my way!" Mr. X says screams at Steve. "You are not the boss here. I can tell if someone is running things, and you are not it. Where is your boss man?"

Within seconds, fifteen agents and police come out of the shadows and grab them at gunpoint. They didn't have a chance, and they knew it. They lay their weapons down and surrender without a fight. As they're being handcuffed, Mr. X yells out that he wants to see the man that stole all his heroin.

"Now that's a wish we can grant," Greg says to him.

Out of the shadows and the back room, Trevor walks out and says, "That would be me." He stops dead in his tracks as he swings at him but is stopped by Greg. "Christopher? You're the man behind all of this? You son of a bitch. Really? I thought you were dead. Everybody thought you were dead. Why? Why?"

Christopher starts to speak but is interrupted by Jimmy.

"Sorry, Trevor. I had a feeling he wasn't dead," Jimmy says. "As I was leaving the precinct today, I received a call from the Cairo museum asking if we misplaced a body. They found a body decomposing in one of the crates that was returned from the historical museum. They never opened them when they were returned because they knew what they were. They were antiquities that were being returned, or so they thought, until something in their warehouse started to smell really bad and they started to investigate and found a body. Their medical examiner had a DNA test done and found out it was a guy named Grant Evans. They are sending all the information to us. This Grant person has a rap sheet a mile long even with

Interpol. That's how they were able to ID him so easily. So I suspected that Christopher was alive and well. Let's introduce the other members of your crew, shall we? This is Rodney, head of security for the historical museum. I wouldn't count on them holding that job for you. Then this one here, I also happen to know this one too. This is Jonathan Foxtrot. We have had minor drug charges against him in the past. Nothing really serious until now. Decided to get up there with the big boys, huh, Jonathan? Don't know this last one, but I am certain we have a rap sheet on him as well."

"I have just one question for you, Christopher. Why get me involved in this?" Trevor says, angrier than he has ever been in his life, he thinks. "What was that game all about anyway? Do you realize that had you not gotten me involved in this, you probably wouldn't be on your knees right now in handcuffs and going away for the rest of your miserable life? I sure hope it was worth it. By the way, just to put your mind at ease, we are going to empty every bank account you have everywhere. Nothing will be safe. You will lose everything, but where you are going, you won't need it. So, Christopher, why?"

"Who knew that you were going to go off and become an FBI agent?" Christopher says.

"Why the hell does that matter? Metro was looking into this while I was away in training at Quantico. It was only a matter of time regardless of all the stupid shit Rodney thought he was feeding Harvey. He wasn't buying any of that crap. And for the record, who actually killed Grant? He was your lead, wasn't he? Or was that all pretend too? So who did kill Grant?"

Christopher looks up at Rodney and doesn't say a word.

"I liked you. My dog liked you and your dog. What a piece of work. I hope you rot in prison." Trevor looks up at Greg and says, "Get this crap out of here. He's polluting the whole building."

Several of the agents in the room listening to all this escorts Christopher and his henchmen out to awaiting vehicles.

"Okay, everyone, that's a wrap," Dave says. "Everyone did great. Guns were drawn, but no one fires a single shot. That's what I call a successful operation. Thanks, everyone. Great job all around. Make sure you send some agent to that holding room and help Logan get all of those men to the waiting vehicles."

Trevor is still just fuming. He can't believe Christopher deceived him so masterfully. This is the guy he wanted to have a relationship with. He was generally sickened by the fact that he was dead. He felt horrible. "Greg, can I be there for the interrogation?" Trevor asks. "I would love to know more about this idiot's operation. I feel horrible about all of this. Maybe I'm not cut out to be an agent. I mean if I can be deceived this expertly, what future do I have as an agent?"

"Look, Trevor, this was not him deceiving you. It was him deceiving everyone. This was a brilliant operation. It really was. He ran it better than any operation I have ever seen. I've been around for a very long time, and I can tell you, given the same circumstances, I would have been just as deceived. Don't be so hard on yourself. You did great, and you will be a great agent. One of the best. You have to realize this was your very first case. Unfortunately, it also became very personal. That happens sometimes, but you handled it perfectly. Look, you didn't know that it was your dead friend until the eleventh hour. I mean, talk about a kick in the teeth. You did not expect to walk into the room and find the friend you thought was dead all these months. Considering what just happened, I don't know if any of us seasoned agents would have done any differently. When I wanted you to step back behind the door to that other room, it wasn't to hide you from Christopher. It was to prevent him from shooting you for stealing his dope. When we grabbed him, his gun was out and cocked. He could have if we didn't stop him right quick.

"Trevor, you did great. I am very proud to have you on my team. Now go home and get ready for your best friend's wedding. We will hold him in metro's jails until Monday, along with Rodney, Jonathan, and the rest of his henchmen. You go enjoy this weekend. They'll keep till Monday." Greg pats Trevor on the back for a job well done.

"Oh, Greg, can we move the interrogation until the afternoon?" Trevor says. "Jason's hearing about his security agency is on Monday morning. I am his key witness. I am hoping the judge will give him eighteen months to run the agency so he has time to get his license. He deserves a break the way his partner tried to screw him."

"Not a problem. We will start when you get there. We will have him moved to our jails Monday morning so they will be there ready for interrogation," Greg assured him.

"Thanks, Greg. I really appreciate that. I will get there as soon as I can." Trevor continues, "Now it's time for festivities and marriage. I will see you on Monday. And Greg, thank you for everything. I appreciate more than you know the confidence you showed in me during this whole operation. I will never forget it. Good night."

Trevor walks out the door of the hotel. The rest of the agents and police were just finishing up on everything. The prisoners have been taken out of here and off to the metro. Jimmy will have them processed there and held for the FBI and DEA on Monday. They can sit in jail all weekend and contemplate what it will be like spending the rest of their lives in prison. Good for them. Couldn't happen to a better bunch of guys.

Trevor is thinking about all this as he drives home.

Chapter Twenty-Three

"Good morning, Jason. Are you ready to get married?" Trevor says in the phone. "Do you have time to meet up with me before we go to the wedding?"

"I do. I am surprised you have time though. I somehow thought you would be rushing in to witness me getting married and then fly out of here to go back to this big case you are on," Jason says.

"Well, as it happens, this big case I was on has pretty much ended," Trevor says. "The only thing we have left is the interrogations, and that will be Monday after we get back from your hearing. Everybody has been captured and is now in jail. All of the bad guys. We didn't miss anyone. We got everybody all the way up to the boss. They are all in jail and will be going to a federal prison to spend the rest of their lives. A well-deserved end to all of this. I can't tell you about it yet, but I will be able to eventually once this is all done. Because it's technically still an ongoing investigation, I can't talk about it. So lets concentrate on getting you married. What time can we meet? Or did you want to meet before the ceremony at the Madhatter?"

"Well, I have some things to do before we get there. Have you picked up your tux yet?" Jason reminds him.

"On my way there right now to get it. I am hoping it fits and does not need to be altered in any way, or I am screwed. I just have not had the time to pick it up before now," Trevor says as he races for the door.

"Aw, I'm sure it will fit. These guys are pros, and besides, you are a regular size—not obese or even real skinny—so there shouldn't be anything magical about the measurements. It will fit. Trust me. I will be out, getting things taken care of up until about three p.m. Can we meet up at Madhatter then? Will that work?"

"Sure," Trevor says. "I will see you then."

"Bernadette? What time are you going to be here?" Jeanette says into the phone.

"Jeanette, I am on my way out the door right now. As soon as I get there, I will honk so you can come out. We have to get to the hairdresser for your hair and nails. I will be there in less than an hour. My husband will bring the girls later in his car. I am yours for the day. Your appointment isn't for another ninety minutes. We have plenty of time. Seems our bride is nervous on her wedding day. Go figure."

"Yeah, but not for the reasons you would think, and you know it," Jeanette says.

"Yeah, I know it. When is Trevor going to talk to Jason?" Bernadette asks.

"I don't know. Jason said he had some things he had to do before the wedding today, so he wouldn't be getting to Madhatter until about three p.m. He told Trevor that, so I think Trevor was going to meet him there early. I think Jason thinks that Trevor just wants to talk about prewedding stuff with him."

"I'm sure it will be okay," Bernadette says. "Trevor is smart and has a good head on his shoulders. He will find a way to break it to him in a way it stings the least. We should be at Madhatter around 3:30 p.m., so if anything comes out of their talk, we will be there to respond. Hopefully, it won't be responding to him leaving."

"Okay, well, there is nothing we can do about it now," Jeanette says. "All we can do is, how did you put it the other day? Oh yeah, let the chips fall where they may. That's all we can do."

Jeanette says her goodbyes to Bernadette so she can finish getting ready before she gets there. And about thirty minutes later, she hears the honking of a car horn. Bernadette is here. Jeanette grabs her purse and her veil and runs out the door, heading for the driveway.

"Come on, Jeanette!" Bernadette yells out the window. "If we get there early enough, they can start on you before your appointment. Just trying to buy you more time later."

Jeanette jumps in the car, and they drive off to her appointment, which is twenty minutes from her house.

"Okay, let the fun begin," Jeanette says sarcastically.

"Hello," Trevor says to the hostess. "I am here for the Jason Brandt wedding. I am Trevor Andrews. You must be new here. My friends and I come here all the time."

The hostess greets him and shows him to the back room that is going to be used as the groom's room. It's really just a conference room they book for events, but tonight, the two conference rooms they have will be the groom's and bride's rooms, a quiet place for them to get ready before the ceremony.

"Is the groom here yet?" Trevor asks the hostess.

"Yes, he got here a few minutes ago," says the hostess. "He's already in the groom's room getting ready. I will leave you here at the door in case he is changing. He came in with his tux over his shoulder. So he intended to dress here."

"Great. Thanks. I got it from here." Trevor knocks on the door and then enters without waiting for Jason to tell him to come in. "Well, now. don't you look nice? You'd swear there was a wedding going on here. What time is the ceremony again?"

"Four p.m. is when the minister will be here," Jason says. "We can get married as soon as he gets here. According to the minister, the ceremony will be short and sweet."

"Nice," Trevor says. "Jason, there is a reason I wanted to talk to you before you get married. I need you to listen to what I have to say. Let me tell you what I have to say before you respond."

"Trevor, you're scaring me. What's this all about?" Jason says with a lot of trepidation.

"Jason, do you remember the night we met Jeanette?" Trevor says. "You had just gotten kicked in the guts because of what Donald Vernon had done to you. You were a combination of super pissed and depressed, wondering what you were going to do now. I suggested we go out and forget about this for a while. In fact, we came here. And at the bar were these girls, one of which was Jeanette."

"Yeah, I remember. Best night of my life. I met the girl I am going to marry tonight," Jason says with some question on his face as to what this is.

"Jason, the night you met Jeanette, the night you say changed your life, dude, I arranged for that to happen. Jason, I paid Jeanette to meet you and have amazing sex with you that night."

Jason is looking at Trevor with these big 'I don't believe it' eyes. "What are you saying?"

"Jason, she was a high-priced hooker that I paid for you to meet and have sex all night long," Trevor says.

"You what? You mean that amazing sex I have been having with her that night and since is because she's a pro?" Jason is yelling at Trevor now and grabbing his jacket like he is going to tear it off of him. "You mean she is a fucking whore? Goddamn it, Trevor. You bought me a whore, and now I am going to marry her? Are you out of your mind?"

"Look, Jason, I never expected it to get this far. You were supposed to have sex with her that night and go on with life and forget that happened. Instead, you started to date her. And what's more, she wanted to date you. But the chicken was afraid to tell you. So I told her I would tell you, but then I went off to Quantico, and everything got busy. Look, Jason, I'm sorry, man," Trevor says, now hanging onto Jason as hard as he is hanging on to him.

"And that makes it all okay, right?" Jason says as he throws Trevor halfway across the room and storms out, screaming down the hall for Jeanette. "Jeanette?" he screams for the whole building to hear him. He is so hopping mad right now. "Jeanette!" He throws the door to her room open. "Tell me what he said isn't true. Tell me he didn't pay you to sleep with me. Tell me you are not a goddamn whore." He is out of control now. He is screaming mad, and he isn't listening to what she or anyone has to say.

"Jason, listen to me. I wanted to date you because I really liked you from the moment I saw you. I felt a connection to you I never felt before. Everybody has a past some people aren't proud of. But we move on. I'm sorry you don't approve of my previous employment," Jeanette says delicately.

"Your previous employment. Your job. How much did Trevor pay for your services that night? Huh?"

"Why does that matter? Why do you care what he paid me?" Jeanette says.

By this time, Trevor is on his feet and right on his heels trying to soften this a little. Jason has been yelling this whole time and yelling out of control. "Because I want to know. What did he pay you to fuck me?"

"All right, all right. Five thousand dollars," Jeanette replies.

"Did you pay it back to him? Huh? Did you? You did say you felt a connection with me, and you wanted to date me as much as I wanted to date you. So did you pay him back?" Jason asks again.

"No, I did not pay him back. Are you happy? I kept the goddamn money," Jeanette says, starting to get pissed herself.

"Oh, don't even think you get to be pissed about this. If it wasn't a big deal, why didn't you tell me yourself? Why did you make Trevor tell me and on my wedding day of all times? Give me one good reason why I should still marry you? I don't know who I should be more pissed at. You or Trevor." Jason is starting to calm down a little now. He is not yelling nearly as much as he was.

"Jason, if you are going to be pissed at anyone, it shouldn't be Trevor. He was just trying to protect you and give you a night to remember. You did remember it, right? After all, you did want to date me. Have your feelings changed now that you know what I did for a living? For the record, when I fell in love with you, I stopped what I was doing because I wanted to be 100 percent yours. No one else's. Doesn't that count for something? Jason, I love you with all my heart. I want to spend the rest of my life with you. Should it matter what I did for a living before? I know, even after all this, you still love me with all your heart." Jeanette wraps her arms around him.

Trevor and Bernadette take this opportunity to leave and shut the door and let them work this out alone.

"Can I buy you a drink at the bar? By the way, my name is Trevor Andrews. I'm the best man if there is still a wedding," Trevor says, shaking Bernadette's hand.

"Hi, I'm Bernadette. I am the maid of honor, assuming there is still a need for one," Bernadette replies. "I am also Jeanette's younger sister. It's nice to meet you. Yeah, a drink would be great. My husband should be getting here with my two daughters shortly. I really hope they still get married after all of this. I know they still love each other."

"Jason, come on. I know you're hurt that I didn't tell you myself, but come on. I know you still want to marry me. One day, we will laugh about all of this." She is still hanging on to him like he will fall if she lets go.

"Jeanette, I do still want to marry you. I just don't know if I can get past the fact that you fucked men for money. For a lot of money. I guess I owe Trevor an apology. I threw him on the floor like I want to really hurt him, and I don't. I love that big jerk. He's my best friend. Okay, if you promise me, we will never talk about you and your past again. I will try to get past this. In the meantime, I don't want to spend another minute without you, so I guess that means we are getting married. Are you ready, or do you need your sister to help you get finished?"

"I need her for a little work still. I need to fix my makeup. I smudged it with tears. Will you go get them back here? I think they probably went to the bar."

"I will go send Bernadette in here while I apologize to the big jerk. I will meet you in the ballroom," Jason says as he walks out of the room after giving her a kiss and a hug.

"Bernadette, your sister needs your help. She needs help fixing her makeup," Jason says.

"So there is still going to be a wedding then?" Bernadette asks.

"Yeah, there's still going to be a wedding. I will see you in the main ballroom in"—looking at his watch—"fifteen minutes," Jason says. "Dude, I need to apologize to you. I shouldn't have pushed you down like I did. I could have hurt you. I am really sorry, man. You are my best friend, and all you were trying to do was protect me." Jason shakes Trevor's hand.

"You know, Jason, you struck a federal officer. That's technically a felony. I could send you away for a long time for that." Trevor laughs. "But I will let you off with a warning and call it matter of temporary insanity." He laughs even harder now. "I'm just glad you worked it out. Shall we head to the ballroom?"

"Sounds like a great idea," Jason responds as they both head in that direction, Jason with his arm over Trevor's shoulder in friendship.

"I now pronounce you husband and wife," the minister says in conclusion. "You may kiss your bride."

Jason kisses Jeanette in a very passionate kiss and embrace, then turns to Bernadette and Trevor to shake their hands while Jeanette hugs and kisses them both. The party starts at about six and goes until all hours. They have a great time, and when they are ready to go home, Trevor orders them a limousine for their trip back. They decide they were going to live in Jason's house, which made sense because Jeanette's house, even though it is a house, is a rental. Jason owns his house. Well, he and the bank.

Either way, they are moving in there, and Jeanette will be giving up her rental. Next week, their honeymoon will consist of them moving her stuff into Jason's house. They won't be able to go anywhere anyway. Monday, he has that hearing where the judge will decide if he gets to continue to run Sheppard Security Services while he works toward getting his license. Trevor is pretty sure the judge will rule in his favor.

Wow, I have to stop thinking about this stuff while I am supposed to be having a night with my new bride, Jason thinks to himself. *Okay, enough of this stuff. Jason, he says to himself, you need to concentrate on this gorgeous woman next to you.* "Hello, Mrs. Brandt."

"Hello Mr. Brandt."

Epilogue

"Trevor, you don't need to be here, you know," Greg says. "We can handle this. If you think this is too painful for you, believe me, we all understand."

Trevor thinks for a second and says, "I appreciate that, Greg, but I want to be here and listen to what he has to say. I am fine. Believe me, I am so over thinking this jackass was my friend. I will just listen behind the glass. Can I come in there if I feel I need a better explanation?"

"Truthfully, I would rather you didn't. They're bringing him down now, and he should be in the interrogation room in a few minutes," Greg says. "I have no problem with you watching and seeing what he has to say, but don't interfere, Trevor, please?"

"Okay, I will just listen," Trevor says.

"Oh, by the way, Trevor, while we are waiting for them to get him in here, how did it go at court this morning?"

Trevor says, "Great. The judge gave him eighteen months to get his license, which is way more time than he needs. The judge was very sympathetic to what Jason went through and even cursed what Jeremy did to him. He said he wishes he could give him more than eighteen months, but that's the maximum that ruling will allow. He gave him the maximum time he could. Jason was very grateful for that. The judge was being very generous with him. Jason has already started working on the paperwork to get his application in. So the judge granted him a temporary license until he goes before the licensing board. After he gets his application in, that can be anytime after that within a three-month period. Jason is very pleased."

"Greg, Christopher is in the interrogation room now. Ready when you are," Dave says as he makes his way to the observation room with Trevor.

"So, Christopher, shall we begin? Let's start with your role at the historical museum. Let's begin with Grant's death, his murder. Did he even know you were the one in charge, or did he think Rodney was the one running things?"

Christopher thinks for a minute and says, "Rodney was an idiot. Grant knew that Rodney wasn't in charge, but he had no idea that I was. In fact, he threatened to kill me when he was holding me at gunpoint. That's when Rodney decided he needed to die. I was not opposed to that. In fact, it was my idea to put my credentials on Grant's body and for Rodney to identify him as me so everyone thought it was me that was killed. We knew we had to get rid of the body as soon as Rodney left the room with Jimmy."

"How many years have you been successfully distributing drugs out of there, and did anyone at the historical museum besides Rodney know what you were doing?" Greg asks.

"No one had a clue. I needed Rodney to control who saw what in there. So I threw money at him, and he was on board because I found out he was really in bad shape financially. So I knew that giving him a large paycheck was going to get him, and I was right. Rodney is the one that beat and killed Grant."

"Doesn't matter," Greg says. "You are an accessory to the murder. Same penalty applies. You are still both getting life, so it really does not matter to us which one of you actually killed him. Okay, so let's go on to the drug shipments."

Trevor and Jason will return in another adventure.

About the Author

Lawrence Anthony Deiman was born and raised in the Twin Cities of Minneapolis and Saint Paul, Minnesota, to a loving family that would later include five siblings. In his early teens, his father moved the family to Chicago, ill after being transferred there by his employer. After high school, he joined the United States Air Force, and since it was during peacetime, he earned several degrees while attending college, courtesy of the military. After college, he was fortunate to get a career job in his chosen field, the information technology (IT) industry. He, later in his career, met a friend whom he had several adventures with and who inspired stories that he wrote and will continue to write. He and his friend were the key inspiration for the story in these pages.

Mr. Deiman (pronounced "diamond," without the ending D) is currently living in the Phoenix East Valley of the great state of Arizona with his beautiful companion Abigail (Abby), who is his pure white Siberian husky with piercing blue eyes. His immediate family had moved to the Chicago area and still resides there to this day. His parents have since passed away. His four sisters and their families live mostly in South Side, Chicago.

CPSIA information can be obtained
at www.ICGtesting.com
Printed in the USA
LVHW091621181120
672046LV00051B/1158